W9-CNK-494

Daniel's feet froze to the paving slabs.

Briefly illuminated in the light from the French windows, Annie paused, the freshening wind catching the gossamer-fine short skirt of her dress, whisking it upward in a swirl of scarlet, displaying more of those endless, shapely legs.

Desire kicked fiercely deep in his abdomen.

Red for danger.

DIANA HAMILTON is a true romantic at heart, and fell in love with her husband at first sight. They still live in the fairy-tale Tudor house in England where they raised their three children. Now the idyll is shared with eight rescued cats and a puppy. But, despite an often chaotic lifestyle, ever since she learned to read and write Diana has had her nose in a book—either reading or writing one—and plans to go on doing just that for a very long time to come.

Books by Diana Hamilton

HARLEQUIN PRESENTS®

Don't miss any of our special offers. Write to us at the following address for information on our newest releases.

Harlequin Reader Service
U.S.: 3010 Walden Ave., P.O. Box 1325, Buffalo, NY 14269
Canadian: P.O. Box 609, Fort Erie, Ont. L2A 5X3

DIANA HAMILTON

The Bride Wore Scarlet

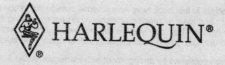

TORONTO • NEW YORK • LONDON
AMSTERDAM • PARIS • SYDNEY • HAMBURG
STOCKHOLM • ATHENS • TOKYO • MILAN • MADRID
PRAGUE • WARSAW • BUDAPEST • AUCKLAND

If you purchased this book without a cover you should be aware that this book is stolen property. It was reported as "unsold and destroyed" to the publisher, and neither the author nor the publisher has received any payment for this "stripped book."

ISBN 0-373-12015-X

THE BRIDE WORE SCARLET

First North American Publication 1999.

Copyright © 1998 by Diana Hamilton.

All rights reserved. Except for use in any review, the reproduction or utilization of this work in whole or in part in any form by any electronic, mechanical or other means, now known or hereafter invented, including xerography, photocopying and recording, or in any information storage or retrieval system, is forbidden without the written permission of the publisher, Harlequin Enterprises Limited, 225 Duncan Mill Road, Don Mills, Ontario, Canada M3B 3K9.

All characters in this book have no existence outside the imagination of the author and have no relation whatsoever to anyone bearing the same name or names. They are not even distantly inspired by any individual known or unknown to the author, and all incidents are pure invention.

This edition published by arrangement with Harlequin Books S.A.

® and TM are trademarks of the publisher. Trademarks indicated with ® are registered in the United States Patent and Trademark Office, the Canadian Trade Marks Office and in other countries.

Printed in U.S.A.

PROLOGUE

ANNIE KINCAID was dying for Rupert to take her home. She just couldn't wait to get out of this place. Normally she loved parties, but this one was giving her a headache.

The level of noise was nothing like as raucous as some of the thrashes she'd been to, so that wasn't the problem. It wasn't the soft music—Vivaldi, she thought—or the thrum of conversation, the occasional ripple of well-modulated laughter that was making her temples pound.

She pushed ineffectually and despairingly at the thick tendrils of wheat-gold crinkly hair which had escaped the chignon she'd so painstakingly created and felt a few more pins slither out onto the gorgeous Persian carpet.

'You should get it cut—one of those new short, sharp styles,' Rupert had once said, 'It's much too wild, makes you look like a bimbo instead of a nine-ties career woman.'

Just one of the niggles that that had piled up, until last night the pile had become a mountain of monstrous proportions.

They'd been at his ultra-modern Marylebone apartment, all steel and leather furniture and waxed wooden floor-blocks. Sitting over the trendy Thai-style supper he'd had delivered from the restaurant round the corner—he always refused to let her cook for him, which annoyed her because she was good at it—she'd casually mentioned children.

'I'd love a huge family. Well,' she'd amended, seeing his sudden frown. 'Three, at least. I never had brothers or sisters, and after my parents died I was brought up by a maiden aunt—the only relative I had. Aunt Tilly thought children were meant to be rarely seen and never—and I mean never—heard!' Her comment, glossing over the loneliness and lovelessness of her childhood, had been meant to be joky, to ease away that frown.

If anything, the scowl on his bluntly good-looking face had intensified. 'Talk sense, Annie. What are you—twenty-four? You've got your career to think of—'

'A secretary,' she had interrupted, to his obvious displeasure. 'That's all I am.'

She didn't want to be a career woman; she wanted to be a mum, the builder and holder-together of a sprawling, happy family.

'You could advance,' Rupert had pointed out. 'If you tried. If you got away from that tinpot import lot you're with. Move to a decent company, aim for personal assistant to a top man. As a matter of fact, there's a secretarial position coming vacant in the research department at the bank. I could swing an interview, maybe even pull a few strings. I do have some clout, you know. Work hard, and it could lead to better things—much better things. The only thing that's holding you back is your attitude.'

He'd poured more wine into her glass. Had he thought it would soften her up, make her more mellow?

'With both of us working after we're married we could afford a seriously decent lifestyle. I don't intend to become the sole provider, missing out on the good life, worrying myself half to death over school fees and fodder bills. Think about it. The job with the bank, that is. As for the other—' he'd shrugged, dismissing her needs, '—we've got another fifteen years ahead of us before we need even consider starting a family.'

He'd pushed the wine towards her over the glass top of the table with the tip of his finger. And smiled his charming smile. The smile that had stopped her in her tracks when she'd first encountered it a few months ago.

Last night it hadn't worked. It hadn't really worked for weeks, come to think of it. And that was responsible for her headache tonight, the way she couldn't be bothered to mingle, enjoy getting to know new people the way she usually did.

Sighing, she remembered the way she had exploded. Told him she didn't want to work in a stuffy merchant bank until she was forty. And said that if he generously allowed her to have a child when she'd reached that venerable age then she'd be drawing her old-age pension before he or she had finished full-time education.

She didn't want to be a career woman with a short, sharp hairstyle, thanks all the same!

She'd called him a selfish chauvinist, and a load of other unflattering names she hadn't been aware she'd known, and stumped out.

And she wouldn't be with him at the party tonight, only he'd phoned her at work—her despised work, she reminded herself—and practically re-invented himself.

'About last night, well, Annie, I apologise. I shouldn't try to force my opinions on you. I love you just as you are, even when you're at your most contrary! I suggest we talk things through, properly. We can go back to my place after the party and discuss everything sensibly.'

With being mad at him, and wondering if their engagement was a huge mistake, she had forgotten about the party his head of department was throwing to mark his imminent retirement.

She'd been wondering if he would have bothered to get in touch with her today if the party hadn't been happening, and was sure of it when he went on, 'Edward has invited the entire staff—at executive level, of course—and their partners. Wives, mostly. It wouldn't do my career prospects much good if I failed to turn up. And they all know of our engagement so they'll expect you to be there. The chief exec is very strong on stable marriages, and I guess that goes for engagements, too.'

She didn't care what the stuffy old chief executive, whoever he was, thought. But she did care about Rupert, and even if they decided that their engagement had been a mistake she wouldn't do a thing to harm him, or his career prospects. She knew how important his career was to him.

So she'd bitten her tongue and ignored his hackle-raising parting comments about taking the afternoon off, visiting a good hairdresser and buying a new dress.

'Something sophisticated rather than the startling

things you usually wear. Something that does justice to your figure, of course, but without being blatant.'

So, for his sake, she'd agreed to be ready at eight, when he would call for her at the flat in Earl's Court she shared with her best friend Cathy, and now she was wishing she had never come. Or at least that Rupert would collect her now, right this minute, and take her home.

Nobody was talking to her and most of the guests looked decidedly stuffy, and some of the women were giving her disapproving looks. She wanted to sit down with Rupert and discuss their future in privacy.

Disorientated by her moments of introspection, she absent-mindedly took another glass of white wine from one of the circulating white-coated waiters. Rupert had abandoned her shortly after their arrival, obviously preferring to talk shop with his colleagues rather than circulate with her.

Or perhaps it had something to do with the dress she was wearing? The choice had been a small rebellion, but important to her. She'd already had her coat on when he'd picked her up, and he had probably been too flattered by her unusual punctuality, thinking she was being careful not to annoy him, to ask if she was wearing something he considered suitable.

Was her stubborn determination to wear what pleased her and not what he wanted her to wear responsible for the way he was ignoring her?

She enjoyed wearing the scarlet silk; it was her favourite. Usually it gave her bags of self-confidence. The halter top dipped low between her full breasts, without exposing too much naked flesh but giving the impression that at any moment it might, and the short, full skirt gave her a feeling of freedom that the svelte little black sheaths all the other women seemed to be wearing like a uniform never could.

And the deep shade of scarlet flattered her unusual colouring, the rich gold hair and her contrasting purply-coloured eyes framed by entirely natural dark lashes and brows.

Besides, to give herself her due, she had struggled for hours to tame her hair. Cut it she would not, not for Rupert or anyone else, and now it was intent on escaping the battery of pins she and—eventually—Cathy had fenced it in with.

Rare melancholy tugged her spirits down. She drank her fresh wine, partly for something to do and partly to console herself. It went straight to her head, reminding her that she'd had nothing to eat since a light salad lunch.

Where in the world had Rupert got to?

She scanned the crowd that filled the impressively large living room of the Hampstead home of the retiring head of department for Rupert's tall, wide-shouldered figure. Most of the men looked alike, in dark dinner jackets, some fatter, some shorter, but none taller.

It was difficult to see, anyway—the smoke-filled atmosphere, the tight knots of guests who broke away from each other, dispersing only to form another knot somewhere else with other people—and her eyes didn't seem to be functioning too well. Everything seemed suddenly out of focus, which didn't help locate her lost fiancé.

Either she needed to see an optician, or the lights were too dim, or the glasses of wine she had so heedlessly swallowed had been too strong. Whatever, she suddenly desperately wanted to find him, make it up—wanted to recapture that sense of joy in being really needed by someone which she'd experienced when he'd asked her to marry him.

And then she saw him. The back view of his tall, elegantly made figure slipping out through the French windows that someone must have opened for overdue ventilation.

She put her empty glass down on the small table she seemed to have spent the whole evening with and began to weave her way through the crowded room, accidentally bumping into a pin-thin woman wearing black silk crêpe, pearls and a frosty expression.

Annie, smiling seraphically, apologised profusely and wove on her way, only one thing on her mind; to find Rupert and say sorry for the vile names she'd called him last night. He surely didn't mean to try to change her, turn her into someone alien—hadn't he said he loved her just as she was?

Perhaps if she could persuade him that his constant fault-finding was ruining their relationship they could get comfortably back on track again. Annie liked the feeling of being loved and wanted; she'd had precious little of it during her growing-up years.

It was past time, she thought as she slid through the French windows, that they tried to recapture what they seemed to have lost in their relationship just lately.

There was a paved terrace. He was standing at the far end; she could just make out his darker outline against the dark December night. It was cold, starless—too cold to stand around suddenly, unexpectedly assailed by second thoughts.

She drew in a deep breath and, scarlet skirts flying, ran across the terrace and flung herself into his arms.

Daniel Faber slipped through the open French windows, stuffed his hands into the pockets of his narrow-fitting trousers and walked to the far end of the terrace.

He needed out of that room. Elegant as it undoubtedly was, it was also stuffy and overcrowded. The sharp December night air was just what he needed.

He drew a litre or two into his grateful lungs and flexed his wide shoulders beneath the smooth silk and alpaca of his superbly tailored dinner jacket. He felt himself begin to relax.

Besides, with him out of the way the others might start to have fun. It couldn't be easy to relax when their chief executive was around. Especially when opinions and betting odds couldn't be openly bandied around in his presence. Everyone was eager to know who would be promoted to the vacant position of Head of Futures when Edward Ker finally retired early in the New Year.

The only two viable contenders were Rupert Glover and Andrew Makepeace. Glover, he felt, had the surer instinct, and an impeccable track record within the bank. Makepeace, though, was steadier, committed to his work and, just as importantly, committed to that pleasant, round-faced wife of his and their two small children. Committed family men made sound employees.

Glover was a horse of a different colour. Until

fairly recently he'd been known as a womaniser—an endless procession of empty-headed bimbos going through his bedroom, apparently.

But a few months ago he'd announced his engagement, surprising everyone. Daniel's PA had passed the information on—Daniel insisted on keeping abreast of internal gossip, keeping his finger on the collective pulse of his staff.

He'd taken his PA's comments on board—the addendum that the token of an engagement ring was probably the only way the bank's Lothario could get the woman in question between the sheets and that the engagement would be lucky to last the week out.

But it had lasted three months. It looked as if Glover had finally decided he'd sown enough wild oats. And, seeing the fiancée in question tonight, Daniel could understand why.

Glover hadn't introduced her, but Daniel had asked around and discovered that the startlingly gorgeous figure in red—standing out like a vibrant oriental poppy amidst the svelte and understated sober colours of the other women—was the fabled fiancée. He could understand why the younger man had kept her under wraps.

That glorious hair—a pity she'd tried, unsuccessfully as it happened, to squash it flat against her shapely head—those pouting scarlet lips and come-to-bed pansy-purple eyes, the voluptuous figure flaunted by that outrageously sexy dress. A combination tailor-made to make any red-blooded male think of steamy nights of passion and a nursery full of babies.

He grinned ruefully at his own lusting thoughts, strong, even teeth gleaming in the darkness. With such a woman for a wife Glover would keep to the straight and narrow, his nose rammed tight against the grindstone. So the odds on his promotion were growing shorter.

And maybe it was time Daniel followed his own rules, settled down to raise a family. He was thirty-six already—time, perhaps. It would certainly make his parents happy. Trouble was, he'd yet to meet the woman he could bear to spend the rest of his life with.

The cold air was seeping through his clothing, cooling his skin. He'd give Ker's thrash another twenty minutes then take his leave. And if he could get to the fabled fiancée without being waylaid by sycophants, he'd introduce himself, discover if her voice was as sultry and exciting as her appearance.

He turned to head back in, then his feet froze to the paving slabs. Talk of the devil!

Briefly illuminated in the light from the French windows the Fabled Fiancée paused, the freshening wind catching the gossamer-fine short skirt of her dress, whisking it upwards in a swirl of scarlet, displaying more of those endless, shapely legs, a tantalisingly brief glimpse of scarlet panties.

Desire kicked fiercely deep in his abdomen. He controlled it. High time he settled down, he mocked himself, if he got horny at the sight of a pair of nicely rounded thighs separated by an intriguing scarlet triangle.

Red for danger.

Just how dangerous he was to discover, as flying feet on impossibly high heels propelled that curvy body right up to him and into his arms.

His nemesis exploded from the dark night in a rustle of silk, a cloud of some heady, musky perfume, a halo of wild tumbling golden hair and a sweetly soft body pressed close to his—a delightful, insistent closeness that rocked him back on his heels, making his arms go out to fold tightly about her, making his head spin, his senses reel.

He could feel the pulsing beat of her heart beneath the seductive, pouting breasts that were so voluptuously pressed against the unyielding rock-hardness of his chest, could feel the warmth of her belly as she wriggled against his pelvis, feel himself harden with startling immediacy, feel his control do a runner as her arms curled up around his neck, pulling his head down to hers.

He didn't need any urging. As his mouth homed in unerringly on the moist pout of her lips instinct slammed the door of his mind on the harsh reminder that this was Glover's woman.

The kiss—the fevered stroke and counter-stroke, the delving, subtle exploration, the moist, receptive sweetness of her, the small slender hands curving now to shape his skull, his own hands moving instinctively to take what he craved; the glorious weight and urgent softness of the breasts that literally peaked into the seeking palms of his hands—made his mind explode in wild psychedelic patterns of light.

This was elemental, untamed woman. And he wanted her—wanted her here, now, again and again.

The sinuous movement of her body against his made him shake with the fiery desperation of his need. Then the small cry she gave, almost of shock, handed him back enough control to still the caressing move-

ments of his hands, to control the urgency of his need
to uncover those desire-swollen globes and suckle her.

The small hands were pushing determinedly at his
chest, and a slow gleam of brightness as the moon
broke through the cloud cover showed him wide dark
eyes drenched with shocked understanding.

For a moment her body quivered in his arms, and
then she turned and sped away as quickly as she'd
come to him, leaving him to spend the next ten
minutes getting himself back in control, castigating
himself bitterly for being such a goddammed fool.

Thirty-six years old and he'd reacted to her initial
embrace like a sixteen-year-old adolescent overdosed
on testosterone. Wryly, he guessed his body was trying to tell him something—like it was high time he
entered a long-term relationship, preferably marriage?

And far from envying young Glover his choice of
a future wife, he pitied him now. What the hell had
she thought she was doing? Offering him partial use
of her admittedly gorgeous body in the hope that having had a taster he'd promote her fiancé to head of
department in the confident expectation of getting
payment in full on delivery?

The unmistakable look of shock in those lovely
eyes must have been brought on by the knowledge
that they were both reaching the point of no return.
That she'd been good and ready for him he had no
doubt. His experience wasn't vast, but deep enough
to know the signs. Had Rupert Glover's future wife
been afraid she might deliver the goods before he'd
been teased enough, been driven wild enough by con-
templating the pay-off to promote her future husband
over his rival?

He felt sorry for the poor devil!

CHAPTER ONE

UNTIL they left the motorway at Swindon, heading roughly north-west for Herefordshire, Annie had been feeling fine, enjoying the trip, the early warmth of the summer sun.

Mark Redway, her boss, drove the open-top MG Sports superlatively well, and he'd picked her up from her flat almost at the crack of dawn to beat the inevitable build-up of traffic at the start of the Bank Holiday weekend.

She loved the feel of the breeze in her hair, tossing it into a crinkly mane, loved the warm touch of the late-August sun on her arms and face.

But.

'I'm beginning to get cold feet.'

'You? Never!' Mark smiled his very white smile, gave her a glancing look from dancing hazel eyes. 'Anyway, you agreed. And they're all expecting you and looking forward to meeting you.'

'That's not true, for a start,' she objected, wondering what madness had induced her to go along with his hare-brained plan. 'The looking forward to meeting me bit. Your poor parents will be dreading having to put up with me for the best part of three days and will hate me on sight—see me as a threat to their plans to get you to walk up to the altar with poor Enid. And she, poor girl, will feel absolutely gutted.'

'And don't forget my big brother in your list of all

17

the "poor" people who will get mental indigestion at the sight of your gorgeous self!' He was openly laughing at her now. 'It is the object of the exercise, don't forget.'

As if she could! Trouble was, Mark was too persuasive for her own good! 'Pack plenty of stunning clothes,' he'd said. So she had. She adored lovely clothes, and could wear what she wanted to now, because Rupert was no longer around to wither her with his disapproval.

For the journey she'd chosen a nifty pair of peacock-blue silk very short shorts, with a matching sleeveless shirt arrowing down to her deep cleavage and tied in a knot just beneath her breasts. And she loved her new high-wedge sandals and big owly sunglasses...

She sighed, sounding stricken, and Mark pulled onto the forecourt of an old, ivy-covered roadside inn and stated, 'Breakfast. It will help calm you down. And then, if you've still got cold feet, I'll drive you straight back to London.'

He looked as if he really meant it. She followed him over the cobbled approach feeling awful, because she had promised, hadn't she? She hated letting people down, and never did, if she could help it. But she couldn't help feeling sorry for Enid, who was in love with him, and his parents who were so anxious to see him settle down.

Annie hadn't expected to be able to eat a thing. But after relishing the delicious crispy bacon and scrambled eggs she knew that not even a guilty conscience could curb her healthy appetite.

And the coffee was good, very good, and as Mark

poured a second cup for them both he said, 'Look at it from my point of view. I didn't ask Enid to fall in love with me, or to "Save herself" for me, as Mum so archly puts it. She's your age and never had a boy-friend—and I guess that makes me feel guilty. But, dammit all, I shouldn't have to!'

He looked so grim. Annie couldn't help but sympathise. Only a week ago, after a particularly hectic day at the Threadneedle Street head office of his im-port/export business, he had invited her to his parents' home for the August Bank Holiday weekend. It co-incided with his mother's birthday, and, as with any family gathering, he'd told her resignedly, Enid Mayhew would be there, gazing at him with adoring eyes and following him around as if tied to him with invisible string.

The daughter of a near neighbour, she'd had a crush on him since she wore gymslips and pigtails and braces on her teeth, and his entire family—including his rather terrifying-sounding big brother—thought Enid eminently suited for the part of tying him down, putting a curb on his wilder schemes and generally domesticating him.

'If you appear as my guest—five-four of gorgeous curves, dressed to knock their eyes out—they might all get the message,' he'd said. 'Let me alone to get on with my life. I love them all to pieces, but I want them off my case. I'm sick of them throwing Enid at my head!'

It hadn't seemed too much to ask then, but now, cradling her cup in her hands, savouring the strong dark brew and watching his gloomy expression with sympathy, she asked, 'And what do you feel about Enid—as a person?'

At first he looked as if he didn't understand the question. Then he shrugged. 'She's fine. I'm very fond of her. She can be good company when she forgets to moon over me, and there isn't a mean bone in her body. But—' he set his coffee cup down with a clatter '—that doesn't mean I want her tethered to me like a whopping great anchor. I want to fly high.'

He already had, Annie thought, but wisely held her tongue. His business wasn't the tinpot affair Rupert had scathingly called it. Business was booming and, ironically, two months after she'd broken her engagement, Mark's assistant had left to set up a PR consultancy and she had been chosen to take his position at a hugely increased salary.

So it seemed that without even trying she had become what Rupert had wanted her to be. A career woman. Certainly she had put all her fond ideas of marriage and a family on hold.

She wouldn't let another man into her life until she was sure his aims were the same as her own.

She wouldn't let another man get close to her until she could find one who could make her senses sing to sweet wild music, just as...

But she was not going to think about that, because whenever she did embarrassment sent her into a state resembling shock, all bound up with a decidedly uncomfortable riot of clamouring hormones.

Discovering that the stranger she'd leapt on had been none other than the chief executive of the bank, Daniel Faber, had given her screaming inner hysterics, and Rupert's slagging off as he'd driven her home on

that dre...
her dress...
corner, t...
just what...
out of her...

So she...
his family...
being force...

'I guess...
Mark said gloomily...
Mum would...
too fond of...
and a bouque...

Any man who...
vote. And she knew how awful it was when people
tried to turn you into something you could never be.

Annie stood up from the table, smoothing the soft silky shorts over her curvy hips, settling her big round sunglasses back on the end of her neat nose. 'I'm on. Crisis over. So lead the way and tell me something about your home county. All I know about Herefordshire is that it's crammed with black and white Tudor houses...'

Mark's family home wasn't one of the timber-frame houses the county boasted but a mellow stone rambling affair, surrounded by trees in heavy, late summer leaf. Hot sunlight beamed down from a cloudless sky and a pack of dogs of all shapes and sizes streamed from the open door in welcome.

Mark, retrieving their luggage, said, 'If you want to get Dad on side, admire his roses. Since he retired, the garden's given him a new lease of life. And if you

praise Mum's cooking and clear yo...
give you anything.'
Anything? Even stealing...
away from the so-suitable...
Annie he wouldn't go...
item, or make adv...
stated that her p...
because of th...
taken a gi...
woman...

...ur plate she'll for-

...her dress, her smile...

...her beloved younger son
...Enid? Mark had promised
...so far as to say they were an
...nces—public or otherwise. He'd
...esence as his guest would be enough
...way she looked, and because he hadn't
...home since his college days—the type of
...he socialised with in London wasn't the type
...ke home to meet the family. Nevertheless, she
...as getting cold feet all over again, agonising over
whether her shorts were too skimpy, her top too revealing.

Bending down, she greeted the tide of dogs to hide
her misgivings, wishing she were back in her Earl's
Court flat, listening to Cathy rave about her latest boy-
friend or discuss the merits of the newest fad diet.

'Annie, I'd like you to meet my parents.' Mark's
voice, laid-back as ever, had her shooting upright.
Hopefully they'd relate the flush she could feel creeping all over her skin—every exposed inch of it—to
the enthusiastic licking the dogs had bestowed on her.

Mr and Mrs Redway were both somewhere in their
sixties, his mother comfortably plump, his father tall-
ish, sparish, very much an older version of Mark himself, his curly nut-brown hair greying, his hazel eyes
hinting at a smile that had gone into hiding at the
moment.

The greeting she received was nothing if not polite.
Too polite, Annie thought, cringing.

Then, 'Take your things up, Mark. I'll show Miss
Kincaid to her room. And Father, fetch Enid from the

kitchen; we have time for a drink before lunch.'
Mark's mother turned to her son, her smile wistful.
'The dear girl's making preparations for the buffet
this evening. She refuses to let me do a thing. So
thoughtful—as always.'

Maternal frost enveloped Annie as she followed her
reluctant hostess up the twisty stairs, along one corridor then down another—as far from Mark's room
as she could possibly get, she guessed.

Annie felt like turning tail and running, but when
the older woman paused, pushed open an ancient oak-
board door and said, 'Your room, Miss Kincaid. I do
hope you'll be comfortable,' she grabbed her slipping
courage by the edges, decided to be herself and not
the threatening *femme fatale* that her boss thought his
family would see her as, smiled warmly and insisted,
'Call me Annie. It's awkward, isn't it, when strangers
descend on you? I was brought up by an elderly aunt
who had to have a week's notice, preferably in writing, before anyone dropped by for afternoon tea! And
by the way, many happy returns of the day.'

'Oh—Mark must have told you!' The blue eyes
crinkled with pleasure and Annie nodded, her smile
widening.

'Of course he did. He wouldn't have missed your
birthday for the world. You know,' she added confid-
ingly, 'although he likes to fly high and far, the hom-
ing instinct's very strong. He'll always come home to
roost.

'I was going to bring you flowers, but he said
they'd have wilted long before we got here.' She
walked further into the room—pretty and airy, rosy
sprigged wallpaper, its delicate pattern repeated on the

curtains and bedspread. 'I don't know your tastes, but I remembered Mark once mentioning your weakness for Belgian chocolates.' She bent and opened her weekend case, scrabbling around for the gift-wrapped box, uncomfortably aware of the brevity of her vividly coloured shorts.

But when she turned and extended the beribboned package there wasn't a hint of disapproval on her companion's comfy face.

'How kind, Annie.' She took the gift. Then, after a tiny pause, asked, 'Have you been seeing my son for long?'

Annie wasn't going to lie to this patently nice woman. 'I work for him. We're friends. Nothing more than that.'

If he could hear her, Mark would probably fire her on the spot—or reduce her salary by half. But Annie wasn't into subterfuge and there wasn't much she could do about it. Whether his mother believed her or not was another thing. But at least the older woman did seem more relaxed.

'Come down as soon as you've freshened up. There's a bathroom right opposite. We'll all have drinks out in the garden—out of the front door, turn right and you'll find us. Dan should be home any time now, and then we can have lunch.'

'Dan' would be big brother, Annie thought, the confidence engendered by being her natural self seeping out of her as soon as she found herself alone.

Meeting the lovelorn Enid would be the next hurdle. She'd rather not jump it, would rather skulk in her room.

She wondered whether to change and decided

against it. Whatever she put on she'd still be noticeable. Unpacking took five minutes, washing and renewing her make-up—sunblock and her usual scarlet lipstick—took another five, while brushing the tangles out of her windblown mane took ten.

Irritated with the whole situation now, she dropped her brush down in the clutter she'd already created on the pretty Victorian dressing table and headed for the door. Only another forty-eight hours or so to get through, so she'd just have to grin and bear it—and remind herself to harden the mush that passed for her heart if her boss ever asked her to do him a favour again!

Halfway down the twisty stairs, feeling sick, still trying to remind herself of exactly why she had agreed to come here as Mark's weekend guest, she felt very ill indeed when she recognised the austerely handsome face and power-packed frame of Daniel Faber as he suddenly rounded one of the quirky bends in the sixteenth-century staircase.

'I've come to bring you down. Everyone thought you'd probably got lost. This house is something of a warren!'

But Annie had already subsided in a heap, sitting down on the nearest tread because her legs had given way, muscle and bone turning to water.

Perhaps he wouldn't recognise her. It had been dark out on that terrace. They hadn't been introduced at the party, either. And she and Rupert had left before he'd come back into the room. She'd made sure of that! And the embarrassing happening *had* been more than eight months ago...

'Just what the hell are *you* doing here?'

Annie gave a faint groan. As soon as he'd had a
proper look at her, he'd recognised her all right—and
the quietly rasping tone told her he didn't remember
their brief encounter with any pleasure whatsoever!

But then, neither did she, she reminded herself
bracingly, gingerly hauling herself back to her feet,
hanging onto the banister. And even though it had
been she who had hurled herself at him, he hadn't
passed up on the opportunity to kiss her back—he'd
done more than that, too, she recalled, righteous anger
momentarily quelling severely intense embarrassment.

'I'm here as Mark's guest, as I guess you must
already know. Surely you were told who to fetch.'

Proud of her cool tone, she made the mistake of
raking her eyes over him, slowly, from top to toe. And
once she'd started the appraisal she couldn't seem to
stop.

How she could ever have mistaken him for Rupert,
even in pitch-darkness, she would never know. Long
legs encased in cool cotton chinos, topped by a body-
hugging black T-shirt—his superb physique owed
nothing whatsoever to expensive tailoring.

At six feet, Rupert was tall, but Daniel Faber could
give him a good three inches. Plus, he was far wider
in the chest and shoulder region and narrower in the
hip. But she *had* known the difference hadn't she? her
ever-active conscience reminded her, bringing hot colour to her face.

As soon as his mouth had covered hers she'd
known. And hadn't been able to resist the startling
effect of what the intimacy of his lips and hands had
done to her.

His dark-browed frown made a deep cleft between

the smoke grey eyes as he returned her minute scrutiny, as if mentally stripping away the silky shorts and top was something he had to do but didn't want to.

'I've only just arrived,' he said through the slow build-up of sizzling tension. 'Dad took me aside and told me Mark had brought a woman guest, that you'd been put in the rose room. He didn't tell me who you were. I took it on myself to fetch you. I wanted to judge for myself how serious Mark might be about you. None of us are entirely happy about the situation. Now I know who you are, I'm furious.'

He looked it, too. Quietly and coldly furious. So he was the adoring Enid's champion, too. Mark had implied as much. Yet her brow furrowed. 'How can you be brothers?'

'Half-brothers,' he corrected impatiently. 'My mother remarried after my father died, and a year later Mark arrived. At the time of the marriage I was eight years old. Old enough to know I wanted to keep my own father's name.'

So he'd been a self-opinionated little boy, too. That figured. Her body was still tingling almost painfully where his eyes had wandered, and she'd had more than enough of this pointless and potentially embarrassing conversation.

She said, 'Shall we join the others before they send the dogs to find us?' and watched his wickedly sensual mouth curve cynically as the steely eyes stabbed her, reaching right into her soul and hurting it.

'And we wouldn't want anyone—Mark especially—to think we were doing anything we shouldn't, would we?'

Flinching at the taunt, Annie willed her legs to stop

shaking, held her golden head high and pushed past him. The weekend had barely begun and it had already turned into a nightmare. She had hoped she would never come face to face with Daniel Faber again, telling herself that even if she did, he wouldn't recognise her.

Now the worst had happened. Face to face with him and not only had he recognised her, he was rubbing her face in her indiscretion. Would he tell his family? Make a joke of it? Or would he make something darker out of a simple mistake?

Only it hadn't been a mistake. Not after his arms had closed around her, his lips making demanding love to her mouth.

Just thinking about it made her face go hot, and a gasp of shock, charged with wicked excitement, burst from her as he caught her hair with one hand, twisting the length of it round his wrist, forcing her to turn back, face him.

'I can't stop you being a menace to the male sex. But don't mess with my family, Annie Kincaid.' Another slight twist of his wrist and she was closer to that tough male body. The harsh, handsome face bent over hers, his breath sweet and clean. So close she could feel his body heat, his power, his contempt. See that contempt in the dark grey eyes.

The contempt withered her; she fought against it, a battle twinned with the crazy desire to get closer still, to touch and be touched, to feel the long, hard length of him against her soft, receptive female curves.

She wanted to tell him he was mistaken, too. She was no man-eater. But that would be giving his jaundiced view of her a credibility it didn't deserve.

Desperately trying to clear her head of the accumulated muddle he had created, she narrowed her eyes at him.

'You're overreacting, Mr Faber. If what happened that night—and it was only a kiss, remember—affected you so strangely, then I'm sorry. But that's your problem. There's nothing I can do about it.'

The moment the words were past her lips she knew she'd said the wrong thing. The sudden hiss of his indrawn breath, the dark glitter of his eyes, told her that her piece of bravado had been taken as a challenge.

Too late to retract now, though. The damage was done. And more was to come as that sensual mouth came down on hers, his tongue diving deep between her parted lips with instinctive, bred-in-the-bone male possession.

And just as suddenly, just as she recovered from the stunned shock of engulfing excitement, her blood fizzing dizzily through her veins as she began a feverish response, he put her away, his hand sliding through her hair, right through the thick and crinkly golden length of it to where it tapered to a curling point in the small of her back.

'Nothing you can do about it? How about carrying on where we left off? When I feel like it,' he drawled. 'For now, though, go on down to lunch. And remember, I'll be watching you. There isn't a corner you can hide in without my eyes finding you.'

Lunch? An impossibility. How could she swallow a thing? She pretended to, though, because to do otherwise would let him see he'd won, ruined her appetite, made her needle-sharp-aware of every inflection of his voice, every flicker of those enigmatically veiled eyes—those watching eyes.

The table in front of the birthday girl had been piled with gift-wrapped packages. Molly Redway indeed *looked* like an excited girl as she tore through paper and sent satin ribbon bows flying to cries of, 'Just what I wanted! Oh, how lovely!' and, 'How did you know I yearned for new driving gloves?' She laid the supple kid leather against her flushed cheek and Daniel said, affectionate amusement curling through his voice, 'You hinted often enough, Ma! Glad you're happy with them, though.'

And her husband reached across the table and squeezed her hand. 'We made notes of all the hints, jotted them down, and then decided who should make you a gift of what!'

Annie slumped gratefully back in her seat, thankful for the distraction. At least Daniel Faber's carefully guarded eyes had something else to focus on right now. And Enid Mayhew had been a revelation.

She was lovely. Slender, with cool, aristocratically beautiful features, her dark hair cut short, soft tendrils framing her face and curling against her long white neck.

Surely any man would be bowled over if such a gorgeous creature professed herself in love with him? So what was wrong with Mark?

Covering her untouched salmon mousse with her vast paper napkin, Annie thought she knew why Mark backed off and hid when most men would jump through hoops of fire to gain the interest of such a beauty. Enid made her adoration far too obvious—

had been doing so, apparently, since she was at school.

Unlike his half-brother—who would greedily take whatever offer presented itself, as witness the way he had responded to her mistaken embrace on that dark December night, and then vilify the woman in question—Mark was a hunter. He would want to pursue, make the woman he wanted want him back, not hand him everything on a plate.

It was all there in her beautiful expressive eyes, in the way those same eyes had misted, the soft lips trembling, when they'd been first introduced, in the way the girl had avoided looking at her ever since.

Annie ached to tell her that she was going about everything in exactly the wrong way. That she, Annie, wasn't what Mark wanted her to seem. But how? When? Since she'd joined the others for pre-lunch drinks on the terrace Mark hadn't left her side, and Daniel had done what he'd said he would. Watched her. Watched her until her skin prickled and her nerve-ends screamed. There seemed little hope of snatching a few private moments with the other girl.

'You've done something to your hair,' Mark commented, one brow quirked to where Enid sat at the far end of the table.

He was sitting far too close to her, and his voice made Annie jump. She'd be fainting at the sight of her shadow next, she thought weakly, wide eyes taking in the other girl's pretty blush.

'I—I had it cut.' She flicked the end of her tongue over her lips. 'I—it was too long and heavy. Hot.'

So she got practically speechless whenever the love of her life bothered to notice her, did she? Annie thought, then saw everyone—except Mark—looking at her own heavy, riotously curling mane and felt herself blush, too. Though not so prettily, she was sure.

'Suits you.' Mark sounded vaguely surprised, and Enid shot to her feet, her mouth quivering.

'I'll clear away.'

'You'll do no such thing!' Molly Redway was adamant. 'You spent all day yesterday and most of this morning in the kitchen. Father, why don't you take everyone on a tour of the garden while I stack the dishwasher? Mrs Potts is due to arrive soon. She's broken her rule of never working at weekends because of this evening's party...' Still chattering, she shooed everyone out of the cool, elegant dining room, through the French windows and into the late August heatwave.

The gardens drowsed in the sun, the trees, heavy and sleepy, casting islands of welcome dark green shade, the harsh light bleaching the rose blooms of colour. Conversation was desultory, movements slow in the summer heat.

A normal family taking mild exercise after lunch. Only this wasn't normal. There were muddles and undercurrents swirling just beneath the surface—forerunners of change. Annie had the feeling that she was some kind of catalyst, and hated it.

At her side, Mark took her hand and Annie, her miserable thoughts on another plane entirely, didn't really notice until his fingers tightened, hurting her. Annoyed with him, she tugged away.

He'd promised there'd be no touching, no lying, that her presence alone would be enough to convince them all that there was no chance at all of him suddenly doing what everyone thought was right for him—settling down to married life with Enid.

Seeing his brother take Annie Kincaid's hand, right in front of Enid's distressed eyes, Daniel decided something had to be done.

He'd been a fool to think a warning would be enough. 'Don't mess with my family,' he'd said, and meant it. But women like Annie Kincaid didn't heed warnings. They used their sexuality to get what they wanted out of life.

She was here with Mark, and yet after only the slightest hesitation she'd responded to that kiss of punishment on the stairs. If he'd carried on, instead of putting her away, he could have taken her back to her bedroom, stripped off the tantalising wisps that were supposed to pass as clothing, stripped her down to her luscious, willing flesh and taken her, possessed her.

And she would have revelled in it.

Disturbed by the way his thoughts were beginning to affect his body, he fell in step beside Enid and began to talk horses, which was her other passion, his mind only half on the conversation.

The poor kid had been in and out of the house since her early teens, had become like one of the family. Mark was a fool if he couldn't see that Enid was worth a thousand Annie Kincaids—cheap baggages with their big and beautiful eyes on the main chance brought nothing but trouble and grief. He wouldn't want his brother hurt in that particular fire.

Normally he would have said that Mark was old enough, smart enough, to look out for himself. But instinct told him that once Annie Kincaid got a man in her clutches she would twist him around her pretty fingers until he bled. Then toss the besotted wretch aside if a better prospect appeared on the horizon.

He'd seen it happen with Rupert Glover. He was not going to stand around and wait for it to happen to Mark.

It was going to be up to him to do something about it.

The opportunity to have a heart-to-heart with Enid came far more easily than Annie could have hoped for.

After taking Mark on one side—hustling him out of sight after a strained afternoon tea on the terrace—she'd pointed out that getting physical hadn't been part of their agreement—she didn't like touching, not even something relatively innocuous like holding hands, if she wasn't serious and committed.

Mark thought she was mad, and she could have slapped him for the scornful derision on his face. Slapped herself, too, because who the heck did she think she was kidding?

The arrogant, bloody-minded Daniel Faber only had to touch her to make her want to do whatever he wanted her to do.

And the only thing she was serious about as far as he was concerned was the fierce and futile wish that they had never met. And committed? As if!

She and Mark had sat grumbling at each other on a bench behind a potting shed at the far end of the garden for much longer than either had realised.

'Good Lord!' Mark shot to his feet. 'We're meant

to be changing for this evening's bash.' He grabbed
her hand and tugged her upright, then dropped it.
'Forgot. Look but don't touch! Though I presume I'll
be allowed to dance with you later tonight? It would
look a bit odd if we didn't.'

'Dance?' She had to trot to keep up with his headlong pace. 'Isn't that a bit over the top for a family
birthday party?'

'You don't know Ma's parties! She's a gregarious
creature and is best friend to everyone in a ten-mile
radius! And they're all invited to celebrate her birthday. Hence the buffet. And the early start so those
with young families can join the fun. After they go—
around nine—it all begins to swing. At least we'll
have tomorrow to recover!'

Annie had already made up her mind to head back
to London tomorrow. She'd phone for a taxi to ferry
her to the nearest train station and Mark would be the
last to know. She'd invent some pressing and urgent
reason for not staying on, so as not to give offence to
the Redways.

She really couldn't endure another day pinned
down beneath the insufferable censure of Daniel
Faber's smouldering eyes, she thought, hurrying along
the corridor to her room, meeting Enid as she emerged
from the bathroom opposite her doorway.

'Oh.' Enid did her best to smile, but Annie saw the
lovely face go pale, heard her voice wobble as she
said, 'We all thought you and Mark had got lost. You
were missing for so long.'

'Just talking,' Annie said breezily, knowing the
other girl didn't believe it, knowing that the other
members of the family wouldn't, either.

'Oh.' Again the wobbly attempt at a smile. 'I'm sharing your bathroom. I hope you don't mind. Staying overnight. Molly's parties go on and on.'

This was the golden opportunity, and Annie meant to make full use of it. 'It's time we talked,' she said soothingly. 'My room, or yours?'

Hours later, Annie wondered if anyone would miss her if she slipped away from the increasingly noisy party and went to bed.

After her talk with Enid, when she'd seen comprehension and complicity suddenly gleam in the beautiful blue eyes, she had felt strangely elated, divorced from it all. Let them sort themselves out.

Mark had had no right to ask for her involvement, and she'd had no right to agree. But, one way or another, she'd be out of here tomorrow.

And the advice she'd given seemed to be working. Enid, bewitching in soft jade-green silk, had been dancing with the hunky son of one of the local farmers ever since the first tape had been slipped into the deck. She ignored Mark completely, giving every impression that she was having the time of her life.

'Excuse me, Annie.' As the tempo of the music changed into slow and smoochy, Mark released her from his half-hearted clasp and strode across the floor to claim the woman who was no longer showing the slightest interest in him and far too much in a younger, better-looking guy.

Annie inched towards the open double doors that led to the comparatively quiet hallway. She'd dressed as down as she could, given the stuff she'd brought with her, teaming a floaty white cotton skirt with a

sleeveless black top which had a modest neckline—
well, reasonably modest, she amended as she slipped
over the parquet of the hall, heading for the staircase.

Mission accomplished, as far as Enid was concerned, and only a few more hours to go before she
could make her excuses and leave. Thankfully, Daniel
hadn't asked her to dance. Being held close to that
hard, sexy body, knowing that for some reason or
other he held her in contempt, would have been pur-
gatory.

He'd been watching her, though. Leaning against
an open windowframe at one end of the buffet. His
brooding eyes had never left her. It had given her the
shakes.

Although the night was warm, she shivered. She
wouldn't be able to relax until she was back in her
own small home where she could hole up and forget
her second encounter with Daniel Faber. It had had a
traumatic effect on her. Which was crazy.

'Annie—I want a word with you.' An inescapable
hand clamped around her arm. The touch burnt her
skin. She didn't have to turn to know who it was.

Air rushed out of her lungs, making her heart
pound, and she had to fight to breathe it back in again.

'Loose me,' she commanded thickly, wondering
what it was about this one man that could have such
an effect on her.

Daniel's fingers tightened. 'You know you don't
mean that.'

He swung her round to face him and he was smiling. He frightened her—or, to be more precise about
it, she frightened herself. Her whole body ached to be

held close to his, for him to lower that fabulously sensual mouth and kiss her again…

'But that can wait. You and I need to talk.'

Wait until when? What did he mean? Annie's eyes cast desperately around. She was in some kind of a trap and there was no one to let her out. The remaining guests were in the huge drawing room, cleared of furniture for this evening, dancing or standing in groups talking, eating and drinking. Even if she screamed her lungs out no one would hear her above the music.

'Annie?' A gentle shake, his fingers soft on her flesh now, had her fiercely deriding herself for being such a fool. She'd accused him of overreacting before and now she was doing the same.

'Well?' She couldn't say more. Her tongue felt thick.

'Not here. The noise coming from that room is enough to shake the whole house.'

He slipped a gentle arm around her, and that was her undoing. The smile in his eyes, in his voice, the unexpected gentleness made her whole body quiver as he walked her towards the open main door.

She couldn't think straight, so how could she walk straight? She leant against his body, sighing as his arm tightened around her waist, his strength supporting her, feeling like a thief because she was stealing a few moments of heaven that he had no idea he was giving…

CHAPTER TWO

THE night air was close and sticky as they walked out of the main door and onto the floodlit drive. A sudden gust of hot wind lifted the flirty hems of Annie's skirt around her knees and pressed the fine cotton against her tummy. There seemed no respite from the heat, even outdoors. And the way Daniel's presence made her blood scorch through her veins wasn't helping.

Annie struggled ineffectually with her flyaway skirts and moments later the first few heavy drops of rain fell.

'The wind makes a habit of wrapping your skirts around your waist to tease the male sex—what did you barter to get the elements on side?' Daniel murmured with throaty amusement as another gust lifted the floaty fabric towards the heavens.

Uncalled for. Annie rooted her feet in the gravel, hoping the shadows would hide her furious blush, and Daniel said, 'We're in for a storm. My car's around somewhere in this lot.'

He took her hand in his warm grasp, long fingers wrapping around hers, and tugged her through the guests' parked vehicles until he located his Jaguar, the silver paintwork gleaming under the security lights.

They were tucked inside just a fraction of a second before the heavens opened. 'Right,' Daniel said, and fired the ignition.

'What are you doing?' She turned to look at him,

39

big, bemused eyes dominating her face, then relaxed back against the leather upholstery, reassured by the flicker of a smile caught in the lights from the dashboard.

'Moving to where we won't be disturbed. Fasten your seatbelt.'

Just for a few yards? Annie shrugged and complied. She supposed it did make sense. The ferocity of the rainstorm made visibility almost nil, the wipers barely coping with the sudden deluge. And of course he would want to move his car out of the way of those of the guests who would soon be departing—and it would be a good idea to talk.

Maybe he'd come to his senses and decided his treatment of her had been way over the top. And she would be able to tell him exactly why she'd mistaken him for Rupert at that other party eight months ago.

Clearly there had been some misunderstanding—a misreading of the situation. No man in his right mind could take so decisively and implacably against a woman merely because she'd flung herself at him, kissing him wildly before realising her mistake and taking to her heels! And there was nothing whatsoever wrong with Daniel Faber's mind!

So this would be a good opportunity to sort it all out, wouldn't it?

She would dearly love the antagonism between them to be over. But would all the stinging tension that made the air fizz around them whenever they were near each other disappear, too?

With the departure of antagonism would there be nothing left? Or would whatever it was that made the atmosphere sizzle still be there, to be built upon?

Suddenly she wanted to be able to build something with this man. She felt it like a keen ache, deep inside her. Which only went to show what a fool she was.

Daniel Faber could have his pick. And the type of woman he would choose would be elegant, quite certainly beautiful, and more than likely out of the top social drawer.

He wouldn't choose a nobody like her, not in a thousand years. A nobody with nothing going for her but a bunch of wild hair and a liking for loud clothes.

She sighed and focused her eyes on the rhythmic sweep of the windscreen wipers, then shot him a frowning glance. She'd been so deeply entrenched in her thoughts she hadn't stopped to wonder why it was taking him so long to find a place to park up.

The car was climbing up a steep, narrow lane, the headlights carving a path through the heavy rain. 'Where on earth are we going?' she demanded as he negotiated a sharp bend carefully, then turned the car onto an even narrower, steeper track, where the hedgerows were so high and heavy with water they hung down, scraping the sides of the vehicle with dark, leafy fingers.

'Relax. Almost there.'

That didn't answer her question. She slewed round in her seat, trying to read something from his face. He was concentrating, his features very controlled. 'You said you wanted to talk,' she pointed out warily. 'What's wrong with now? So far you've said nothing.'

He stopped the car. The powerful headlights illuminated a small stone cottage in a raggedy patch of garden, separated from the unmade track by a crooked gate. And then he switched off lights and ignition and there was just the darkness and the beating rain and the rapid thud of sudden anxiety as it pulsed chaotically through her veins.

It got worse as he produced a torch from somewhere and flicked it on. 'Sorry about the weather. We'll have to make a run for it. I'll be right behind you with the torch, so you'll be OK if you watch your step.'

'Make a run for what?' Annie folded her arms across her chest. She was going nowhere. She was stopping exactly where she was.

'For the cottage, of course.' Impatience tinged his voice. 'I don't intend spending the night in the car.'

The night? The *whole* night?

'You have to be joking!' Distrust made her voice sharp and a current of something—fear or manic excitement, she didn't know which—shot through her veins, making her stomach clench. 'Either that or I've missed the point entirely.'

'No joke, Annie,' he drawled, reaching into the rear of the car for a holdall. 'We've fallen madly in lust and have sloped away to spend the night in my private bolt-hole—that's the point of the exercise.'

'You can't mean it!' Annie wailed in shocked outrage. What type of woman did he think she was? Had he marked her unhidden response to both of the times they'd kissed? Given her ten out of ten for effort and decided he was on a winner?

The whole idea terrified her. To her endless shame she just knew that if he'd decided to seduce her, her reckless body would aid and abet him in any way it could!

She wasn't into one-night stands!

'Of course not,' Daniel stated. 'It's the impression that counts. Mark won't be able to believe we spent the night together making polite conversation.' He pocketed the ignition keys. 'Coming? Or do I have to carry you?'

He was out of the car and opening the door at her side before she got her head straight. Mark had persuaded her to be his guest to give the impression they were an item. Daniel had abducted her to give Mark the impression she was anybody's!

She slid out of the car, into the sluicing rain, her body on automatic pilot. She'd go with him because he wasn't a threat. He didn't lust after her; he'd said as much.

'You can't make Mark marry Enid,' she muttered, the rainwater cooling her overheated brain. 'You can't abduct every girl he brings home. You can't run his life for him.'

'He doesn't bring his women home; he keeps them discreetly under wraps.' He unlocked the cottage door and after a moment's hesitation she walked in, drenched by the downpour, dripping onto the coir matting that covered the floor of the small room revealed as he flicked on the overhead light. 'The fact that he brought you home indicates that it's more serious than his usual short-lived affairs. I don't want to see Mark get romantically involved with someone like you.'

Someone like her! Hateful, snobbish wretch! 'He isn't!' she defended hotly, but he wasn't listening, had turned his back on her while he pulled a mobile phone from a side pocket and keyed in numbers. His voice was smooth, laid-back when it was eventually answered.

'It's me, Ma. Annie and I decided we wanted to get to know each other better. So we're spending the night at the cottage—tomorrow and Monday, too. I'll drive her back to town when I go in on Tuesday morning. Let Mark know what's happening, will you? And Ma? Tell him sorry, will you? Tell him it's just one of those things; it just happened.'

Annie stared at his wide shoulders, the hard muscle and bone clearly delineated beneath the clinging wet fabric of his shirt. How dared he give those nice people—his parents—such a bad impression of her? She wanted to leap on him, tear the phone away and tell his mother there wasn't an atom of truth in what the wretch was saying, beg her to ask Mark to come and rescue her!

But, as if reading her intention, he turned, the coldness of his raking glance effectively freezing her to the spot. 'Really?' One dark brow slid upwards now, meeting the damp black hair that fell over his brow. He was obviously surprised by what his mother was telling him. 'Well, it's about time he opened his eyes, I guess.'

He was grinning as he cut the connection and re-pocketed the instrument. 'Mark and Enid were last seen escaping the party, creeping into the privacy of the library, hand in hand. He must have discovered that he prefers quality over quantity.' His grin was slowly wiped away as his eyes made a slow, insulting inventory of her voluptuous curves. Her wet clothes were cocking a defiant snook at modesty, and his eyes were hooded, his face all hard lines.

Annie shook with temper, deep misery and a hateful frisson of sexual awareness. He did lust after her, despite what he'd said. She could see it in the shadowed smouldering eyes, the lines that suddenly bracketed that long, sensual mouth, the jerk of a muscle at the side of his hard jaw.

But his latest vile insults armoured her, didn't they? Involuntarily, her teeth chattered, and his mouth curled in slow, mocking response. 'Tough luck, Annie. Still, some you lose, some you win.' He shrugged impressive shoulders. 'You're on the loose again, but don't try to get your claws into me. The way you responded in my arms earlier told me you wouldn't be averse to ditching Mark and moving on and up the ladder of financial security.'

Daniel turned and tugged the sage-green heavy linen curtains over the window, shutting out the stormy night. For some reason he was unable to look at her pale, bewildered face. Annie Kincaid was surely in the wrong profession. Her acting ability—quite apart from the way she looked—would have taken her far.

He mentally squashed the unwelcome desire to take her in his arms, soothe the look of hurt from those alluring pansy-purple eyes, putting the urge down to twelve months of celibacy. He had no intention on following up, taking what this sexy little gold-digger would doubtless offer, given half an opportunity.

At one time, after he'd learned that she'd dumped Glover, he'd been severely tempted to find her—if only to stop the regularly occurring dreams he'd had. Tormenting dreams of her naked body in his arms, writhing beneath him as they took their aborted wild encounter of that December night to its natural conclusion.

Dreams that had left him edgy, tense, strangely aware for the very first time of an emptiness in his life.

Fortunately, common sense had ruled his hormones. He hadn't known, then, that she'd been working for Mark, had bewitched him, too. Obviously she'd seen Mark as the better prospect, had dropped Rupert Glover flat. That he, Daniel Faber, had failed to follow up on her unspoken yet explicit invitation would have been written off with a shrug of those pretty shoulders.

Annie watched him, too wet and miserable to try to change his opinion of her. It didn't really matter what *he* thought of her. But would Mark believe her when she tried to explain what Daniel had misguidedly done? Or would he believe what his brother had deliberately set out to make him believe?

'How can I face Mark after this?' she asked thinly, and saw him turn back to her, his face blank. 'Embarrassing won't begin to cover it. He is my boss—'

'So Ma told me earlier,' he cut in. 'You could always find another job. With your attributes it shouldn't be a problem.'

Even if Mark had suddenly seen Enid as a desirable young woman instead of a tiresome teenage millstone, it would be better all round if this sexy baggage moved out of his orbit. Daniel had always prided himself on being single-minded, dedicated to his work, but if Annie Kincaid worked for him he didn't like to think how quickly he might give in to temptation. No man would be immune.

Seeing the sudden glitter of tears in her eyes, he relented enough to say gruffly, 'I'll put the immersion on for hot water; you can have a shower later. But for now you'd better get out of those wet things. While you and Mark were helping yourselves from the buffet I went up and threw some of your things in a bag.' He indicated the holdall with a dip of his head. 'I'll get Ma to send the rest of your stuff on. Mark will be able to give me your address.'

Annie stared at the holdall. He'd dropped it on the only means of seating in this sparsely furnished, severely masculine room. Her lower lip quivered. How dared he suggest she get another job? She loved her job, was good at it, enjoyed working with Mark.

Trying not to burst into childish tears, she plucked the small holdall from the battered, leather-covered Chesterfield and followed mutely as he led the way up the narrow flight of uncarpeted stairs that climbed up from the side of the chimney alcove that dominated the tiny room.

At the top he entered a cramped bathroom and came out with a towel. He opened the only other door and pushed the towel at her.

She grasped it, wanting to hurt him back. 'I've never seen such a mean little dump as this,' she said coldly. 'They say you can tell what people are like from where they live.'

'Do they? I really don't give a fig for what people may or may not say. This place suits me, for weekends.' One strongly marked dark brow rose slightly, his mouth quirking with amusement at her childish attempt at retaliation. 'Somewhere to unwind, breathe good country air, but close enough to visit with my folks if I feel like it. So I'm afraid you'll have to endure.' He gave a minimal shrug. 'When I marry I'll have to find somewhere larger.'

The amusement was suddenly wiped away by a darkening frown. 'Dry yourself off and get into fresh clothes,' he said sharply. 'I'll use the bathroom.' And he left her staring at a huge double bed that occupied most of the oak-boarded floor space, leaving only enough room for a bedside table, complete with a shaded lamp, and a tall pine chest of drawers.

So he was going to be married. That figured. It was amazing that some lovely creature hadn't snapped him up years ago. So why did her heart feel as if it had been mangled? Why the urge to cry her eyes out?

She looked around her miserably, desperately needing to be back in her own home. But it was pointless to think of running out into the night and the steadily falling rain.

Spindly high heels weren't designed for steep unmade tracks. And heaven only knew how far she was from the nearest neighbour. So flight, as an option, was out. Besides, now she knew what a sneaky, devious, arrogant bastard he was she would be able to freeze him off if he came over all lustful. Which, she was sure, he wouldn't—not after so insultingly warning her off. In any case, he wouldn't do anything to jeopardise his relationship with his future wife.

The fact that there was only one bed in this dump of a cottage wasn't a problem either. One of them, and she didn't care which, could sleep on that battered old sofa.

Sorted, she thought, with a welcome resurgence of stiffening, and peeled off her clinging damp skirt and top, her skimpy wisps of underwear, then, wrapped in the towel, investigated the contents of the holdall.

He hadn't packed a single sensible thing!

Nothing practical like a toothbrush or hairbrush. Not a stitch of underwear. Simply her favourite oyster satin clingy nightdress—the one with the narrow shoestring straps and daring neckline—a pair of aubergine-coloured flowing silk trousers and the camisole top that went with them. No sign of the matching slimline jacket. No sign of anything else at all.

The rotten louse had hatched his devious abduction plan early on in the evening, had sneaked like a thief to her room and 'packed' for her. Man-like, he hadn't given a thought to the practicalities, just stuffed the first couple of garments he'd pulled out of the drawer into the holdall.

Or had he? Had he, perhaps, deliberately left all her undies, the cotton shirts and shorts behind, wanting her at a disadvantage? She wouldn't put it past him.

Unable to bear the thought of putting her wet things on again, she resigned herself to the silk trousers and camisole top. The soft gossamer-fine fabric clung lovingly to her thighs and tummy—she didn't dare think what it did for her backside—and made the fact that she wasn't wearing a bra decidedly obvious.

Angrily, she took them off and shrugged her nightdress over her head. Normally she loved the feel of the cool satin on her skin. Right at this moment she hated it. It made her far too aware of her own body.

She was going to go to bed, forget about a shower and do the previously unthinkable and retire without brushing her teeth. No way, *no way* would she go begging for the use of a spare toothbrush. No way would she leave this room until the clothes she had worn for the party were dry.

Grinding her teeth, she spread the wet garments out over the foot-board of the bed. And in case he got any funny ideas she would—

But there was no lock to the door, and no chair to wedge under the handle. And she couldn't move the chest of drawers an inch, let alone clear across the room.

Exasperated, she straightened, her cheeks a soft pink, her breasts heaving from her useless efforts to move the heavy piece of furniture, and Daniel pushed open the door and walked right in.

'Get out!' she snapped, the control she'd fought so hard to hang on to flying out of the window, getting well and truly lost in the storm. 'I don't want to be here, but while I am this is *my* room, and if you find that inconvenient you've only got yourself to blame!' She drew in a great lungful of much-needed air and blistered on. 'You think you're omnipotent—deciding who poor Mark should marry—but while I'm here— under duress—you will toe my line. Is that understood?'

She sincerely hoped so. The wretch was wearing a towel loosely slung around his hips and nothing else. His rough-dried hair was sticking up in spikes, which effectively banished the chief executive image, and his lean, hard, perfectly proportioned body was glistening with droplets of water.

He must have just had a shower. A cold one. Suddenly that seemed like a sound idea; despite the rain, the air was hot and steamy.

Instead of doing the decent thing and getting himself out of here, he calmly ignored her tirade, remarking coolly, 'Mark's choice of a future bride is his. I wouldn't presume to put any pressure on him in that direction. But I'm too fond of him to see him get mixed up with the likes of you. I saw what you did to Rupert Glover. And I was on the receiving end of your attempt to cosy up to what you would have seen as a much better prospect while you were still engaged to him.'

He was walking further into the room, his eyes fixed carefully on the chest of drawers, deliberately not looking at her after that first comprehensive glance. She was too stunned to order him out. What did he mean? What was she supposed to have done to Rupert?

Her three-month engagement had been a sobering experience. She had never been able to understand how Rupert had so drastically changed in such a brief span of time. The charming, persistent pursuer had metamorphosed into a petty tyrant, trying to turn her into something she could never be. She had been chillingly reminded of Aunt Tilly, the guardian she had never been able to please no matter how hard she had tried.

No matter how foul Daniel Faber was as a character, no one could deny he was physical perfection. Just looking at the broad, honed structure of his naked back, the wide shoulders tapering down to narrow waist and hips, made her breath go thick in her throat. Touching, actually touching him, sliding her fingers over that warm, satin-smooth skin, would send her clear out of her mind...

Her fingers curled convulsively at her side, her

breasts hardening beneath the scant satin covering. He was pulling worn old denim jeans out of one of the drawers and the towel he was almost wearing was beginning to slip…

With a strangled moan she dived into the bed and pulled the light quilt over her head, partly to hide her own shamefully aroused body and partly to block out the disgracefully male temptation of his.

Muffled beneath the quilt, she saw the room go dark when he clicked off the light, heard the door close. Staying in, or going out?

Her breath held, because she'd forgotten how to breathe, she waited, tense, her body quivering with forbidden desires. And when long moments passed without the dip of the mattress, the sound of his breathing as he joined her in the bed, the warmth of his body as it brushed against hers, she let out a long racking sigh, turned on her back and stared into the darkness, her eyes wide and full of tears.

Daniel lay on the sofa, listening to the silence. The sound of the rain lashing against the windowpanes had been company of sorts, giving him something other than his thoughts to focus on.

Now the rain had stopped, and his uneasy thoughts rattled around inside his skull.

In deciding to release his brother from Annie Kincaid's greedy clutches he'd jumped the gun. According to Ma, Mark and Enid had been like Siamese twins ever since he'd snatched her away from that son of a neighbouring farmer. A nice lad. Cheerful. He couldn't remember his name. He tried to remember, to give his over-active brain something to do other than think about her.

It didn't work. His wretched, sleep-starved brain kept returning to her. The way she'd looked when he'd gone into the bedroom to get fresh clothing. Wearing that slinky clinging nightdress, the dull gleam of the pale fabric so lovingly following every sensual curve and dip of that gorgeous body, those big, big eyes, that wild and wonderful hair, those lusciously pouting lips...

He groaned, wishing he had a pillow to punch, knowing that a pillow wasn't what he wanted. He wanted her, craved that lush and glorious body, wanted to touch, explore, to kiss, to enter. Possess. Own.

He squirmed into a sitting position, elbows on knees, his head in his hands. She was in the room above. There was nothing to stop him going up to her. Nothing at all. Just one touch would be enough to get her wanton little body responding with the enthusiasm he remembered so well from that first encounter.

Her dive beneath the bedclothes had to have been a come-on. An invitation for him to jump straight under them with her. What else could it have been when it seemed she didn't have a modest or virginal bone in her body?

So, no, there was nothing to stop him except his own will-power. And if he hadn't acted the way he had—maybe unnecessarily, he conceded now—getting her here, setting her up so that Mark would see her for what she was and back off with a sigh of relief at his deliverance, he wouldn't be in this position, sleepless on an uncomfortable sofa, dredging up every last ounce of that will-power. Having an almighty battle on his hands.

He'd acted out of brotherly love and genuine concern. He'd seen what her behaviour had done to young Glover. The once pleasant, hard-working, dedicated young man had turned into a long-faced misery it was painful to be around.

At first Glover had claimed that he had broken the engagement after discovering that Annie Kincaid wasn't suitable wife material. After his own encounter with her at Edward Ker's party, Daniel could go along with that. No woman who would wait her opportunity to fling herself at her fiancé's boss was worth knowing.

Then word had got through, via Daniel's assistant, that after joining the usual Friday evening crowd at a local wine bar, Glover had imbibed too deeply, had eventually broken down and admitted that Annie had dumped him. It had shattered him. He couldn't sleep at nights for thinking of that sexy little body tucked up with some other guy. He hadn't named the other man, apparently, either because he didn't know or was too drunk to remember.

The moment Daniel had realised who Mark's weekend guest was he'd known who the other man was. His brother. He'd guessed why she'd jumped out of Glover's bed—jettisoning his engagement ring and breaking his heart on the way—and into Mark's. Mercenary self-advancement. Even if Glover had got his promotion, he would never command the kind of wealth Mark had at his fingertips.

Daniel sympathised with the poor sucker.

Five years ago he'd been down that road himself, bewitched and bedazzled by a woman who had only been interested in his bank balance. It had taken him some time to learn the truth, but when he had he'd developed a self-protective cynicism that armoured him against soft, scented bodies, come-hither smiles and pretty eyes fixed firmly on the main chance.

Or was that armour developing cracks? Wide enough to allow Annie Kincaid through?

Hell, no! No way!

Coffee, hot and strong; that was what he needed. He got to his feet just as he heard the bathroom door creak open, followed by a crash that reverberated through the tiny house. Then a wail of distress. Cut short. Then nerve-tingling silence.

His heart jumped. Had she fallen? Knocked herself out on the pedestal of the washbasin, the edge of the shower stall? He moved, bare feet pounding on the twisty stairs.

She hadn't been able to sleep and had developed a pounding headache. Tension-induced, she guessed, sitting up against the pillows and massaging the back of her neck.

It didn't help. Maybe the louse kept painkillers in the bathroom? It wouldn't hurt to go and look. The rain had stopped some time ago and she'd heard no sound from below for what seemed like hours. The louse would be sleeping, which seemed very unjust.

Slipping out of bed, she padded silently over the floorboards, feeling for the doorhandle and easing it open quietly. She didn't want to wake him. She needed to ignore his very existence, get through this endless-seeming night somehow and demand—yes, *demand* he drive her back to London first thing.

She felt her way across to the bathroom door and pushed it open. It creaked. She held her breath in case the sound had wakened him, then eased forward, feeling a clutch of panic around her heart. She felt for a light switch, then fell over something hard and sharp.

Her involuntary screech would have woken the dead, she recognised as she bit it off in full flood. The day's accumulation of misery, mixed emotions and received insults swamped her. She lay where she was, in a heap, and wept as if she would never stop, couldn't stop, all hope of dignity gone.

The overhead light snapped on and Daniel said sharply, 'Have you hurt yourself?'

What did he care? she thought, wallowing in self-pity. If she'd broken every bone the hurt would be nothing to what he'd dealt out during this awful, awful day.

'Annie—'

His voice was gentler now, and if she hadn't known better she would have said he sounded really concerned. He was kneeling beside her, pushing the upended bathroom stool she'd fallen over out of the way, his hands careful as he pushed the heavy mass of hair away from her face, which only served to make her sob all the harder.

'Tell me where you hurt.'

The capable hands began to move all over her body, and she couldn't stand the gentle exploration for possible damage. She really couldn't! She wanted to tell him: In my heart, you great brute! You hurt my heart! But she didn't.

She snuffled, barely audibly. 'Nowhere. Just knocked my leg. Go away.' And she sat up, hanging her head so that her cloud of hair hid her messy, tear-crumpled face.

'Let me take a look.'

He righted the stool and lifted her onto it, and Annie had to do hectic battle with the senseless desire to wrap her arms around him and cling and cling and go on clinging.

She sat bolt-upright on the stool instead, stiff as a wooden peg, holding her breath while he slid the hem of her nightie up to her knees.

And, as if she didn't already know it, he said, 'You knocked your shin. There's already a sizeable lump.'

The hands that had been holding her ankle slid upwards, curving round her calf, avoiding the grazed area of her shin, and Annie twitched and dragged in a ragged breath as the warmly intimate touch of his fingers on her flesh made heat pool liquidly in the pit of her tummy.

The slithery fabric dropped back down to her ankles. Daniel moved it impatiently back up again, higher this time, well above her knees, pushed himself to his feet and said gruffly, 'A cold compress should help.'

'No. No need.' She stood up. She had to get out of here. The air was fizzing in the confined space. She had to get out because she wanted to stay. Wanted it with a desperation that shocked her. Wanted him to go on touching her.

She had never felt like this before, not even with Rupert—the only man to have ever got beyond her strict allowance of one chaste goodnight kiss at the end of a date. She had been going to marry Rupert, she'd worn his ring, and he'd said it simply wasn't fair on him to keep holding him off.

So she'd capitulated. Not because she felt a desperate need, but because he did. And she'd loved him—or thought she had at the time.

She couldn't say she'd found the experience of sharing his bed very pleasurable. The only emotion she'd felt was a wave of tenderness, a kind of soft happiness because she knew she was doing something right, making him happy, pleasing the man who was going to be her husband. And she had, at last, someone who loved her.

Shortly after that the petty tyranny had begun, and she hadn't let him make love to her again. The more he'd tried to change her, the more withdrawn she'd become—starting to hold him at arm's length, hoping that one day she would find a need for him inside herself.

But she never had. Had only known what real need was like in Daniel Faber's arms.

So she had to remove herself from temptation. Fast.

She wasn't nearly quick enough. She had barely hobbled to the door before he swept her up into his arms.

'I'll carry you back to bed. That bump is obviously painful.'

It was exquisite torment. He was naked apart from the soft worn jeans he'd taken from the drawer, and his skin against hers was turning her to fire. Before she knew what was happening, before he'd crossed the small space at the head of the stairs, her arms had wound around his neck—her head dropping forward into the cradle of his shoulders, her lips finding the salty satin of his burning skin, tasting the heady male astringency of him.

And long before they reached the bed his breath was coming hard and fast. When he lowered her onto the mattress his long body joined hers, and she knew the battle had been lost.

CHAPTER THREE

PASSION was a shared hunger—a hunger she had never known before, and certainly never shared, Annie decided deliriously as he kissed her yielding lips until her head spun round in dizzy circles.

A never-ending circle, spiralling higher and higher, faster and faster, until she thought they would both go into orbit. And then she stopped thinking, simply felt, gave in to a depth of rapturous emotion, an emotion so deep, so awe-inspiring she could hardly believe it was happening.

His exciting male demands turned her body to malleable putty, in turn melting against the taut, hard length of him then writhing impulsively, moving with him, making demands of her own which he met exultantly.

His long hands carelessly brushed aside the tiny straps of her nightdress, exposing the lushness of full, aching breasts—an ache he assuaged as his dark head came down and took each engorged tip in turn into the moist, tugging heaven of his mouth.

His hands moved over her, touching each ripe curve, every secret hollow, touching and lingering, moving until the oyster satin bunched up around her waist and her legs were free to part and wrap around his body.

A convulsive shudder rocked him as he eased away. Annie cried out, a wild cry straight from the heart,

forbidding rejection. And he said her name soothingly, a strange catch in his voice as one of his hands
went unsteadily to the top button of his jeans.

A small gesture of intent. The natural progression
to what they both craved. The taming of the desire
that had sent them out of control. A small gesture, but
enough.

Enough to make her see what was wrong.

Nothing this beautiful, this elemental, could be
wrong—apart from the little matter they were both
guilty of overlooking.

Annie did what she had to do. It took all her will-
power and gave her grief but she did it because there
really wasn't any option. She unwrapped herself from
him and scrunched herself up, folding her arms
around her body to contain the dreadful pain that began in her heart and spread out to every inch of her
body.

'You're going to be married, Daniel. Remember?'
she reminded him thickly.

His lean, sweat-slicked body jerked as if he'd been
shot with a bullet, then went very still. There was
silence for long, aching minutes—silence except for
the sound of his breathing, which he finally got under
control, while she was whimpering inside like a hurt
animal with nowhere to hide, no comfort to take.

So much control that when he slid off the bed his
voice was cold, impersonal.

'I'm indebted to you for your timely reminder,' he
said, and walked out. It was like a cruel slap in the
face. No whispered regrets, not one word of apology.
Nothing.

Annie spent the rest of the night wondering who she hated the most. Herself or him.

Him for turning her pleasant little life upside down, for making her want him as she'd never wanted anything in her nearly quarter-century of living? And the strength of that wanting was even more painfully desperate than that of her remembered ten-year-old self, yearning and weeping for the parents who had been so cruelly taken from her in a stupid, unnecessary road accident.

Or herself for actually desiring, falling halfway in love with a man who, although lusting after her, otherwise thought she was scum, not fit to be near his half-brother for fear of some kind of vile contamination?

At one stage she heard the Jaguar's engine leap to life and scrambled out of bed, over to the window in a panic, in time to see quickly receding tail-lights. So the rat was leaving her here, at the back of nowhere, just disclaiming any further responsibility for her—just as if she were a piece of rubbish he'd tossed in a bin.

Rage made her heart swell, gave her a much needed injection of stiffening. So he'd abandoned her—so what?

She'd show him she could get out of here under her own steam. In daylight she could locate the nearest neighbour, no problem, beg for the use of their phone and call a cab to take her to the Redways' to pick up her possessions.

Facing them wouldn't be easy; she dreaded it. But she had to make herself do it.

She was still trying to work out what she could

possibly say to those nice people to convince them that she wasn't the woman of loose morals their hateful elder son had meant them to think her when, with very mixed emotions, she heard the Jaguar return. On the one hand she'd worked up a good head of steam, was ready and eager to show the rat she could cope very well without him, yet on the other there was a crazy sense of relief. He wasn't, after all, uncaring enough to just abandon her.

When the long-awaited grey drizzly dawn came, heralding a wet Bank Holiday Sunday, Annie was determined to develop a hard shell on her too-tender heart. It was the only way she could emerge from this hatefully humiliating encounter with her heart intact and her emotions safely on an even keel.

She would first go to the bathroom—scene of the beginning of last night's humiliation—and test the durability of that necessary shell by absolutely refusing to allow herself to think of the way she had felt when Daniel had gently eased the satin fabric high above her knees, looking for damage. That had been the beginning of her rapid surrender to the fires of unprecedented desires.

Well, no more. Never again.

So she went, banging doors. No creeping around, trying not to wake him. Why should he sleep when she hadn't had so much as a wink? The shell she needed was growing.

The water was hot and the shower revived her. She rough-dried her hair with one of the fluffy towels and got most of the tangles out with her fingers. Then she banged doors again as she went back to the bedroom to dress.

With a gesture of distaste, she stuffed the satin nightdress into one of the drawers, the flowing silky trousers and matching camisole top following decisively. She never wanted to see those particular garments ever again. They would remind her of him, of last night, of what had almost happened. She surely didn't need that.

She closed the drawer with a bang, shutting them out of sight, and clothed herself in yesterday's underwear, skirt and top, everything still slightly damp and definitely scrumpled.

Annie quelled the sensation of distaste as damp fabric clung to her skin, and refused to despair over the reflection the mirror gave back to her. She looked wild, like a trollop who had spent the night dubiously and was staggering home at dawn.

She didn't care. She wouldn't let herself care. And she clattered down the stairs in her high and spindly heels, stamping into the living room where Daniel was staring out of the window.

He was still wearing the old jeans he'd put on last night and nothing else. Her heart thumped uncomfortably. She would not let herself drool over the perfect line of his long back, the breadth of those rangy shoulders tapering down to the lean waist, the sexy way the soft denim fabric clipped narrow hips and taut male buttocks. She would not! So why did her eyes seem glued to him?

But she was able, thank heavens, to drag her eyes away as he turned from his brooding contemplation of the soggy morning, able to tell him coolly, 'I want to go back to London today. Now.'

'Flatten your feathers. It's already sorted,' he

drawled, sounding sick of her, weary of the situation that had been entirely of his own making. 'The best thing, under the circumstances, is for you to get back to where you came from as soon as possible. I've arranged for a car to collect you. It should be here in just under half an hour.' He drew one hand over his blue-shadowed jawline and tacked on, 'Make yourself a coffee—you'll find packs of long-life milk in the fridge—while I get a shower and shave.'

He was already heading for the stairs in an almighty hurry, as if he couldn't wait to get away from her. As he brushed past her he said, tight-lipped, 'I collected your things in the early hours. I thought it would save someone the trouble of having them sent on. They're in the kitchen. If you're making coffee, make one for me.'

On your bike! Annie thought vehemently, but kept the retort to herself. From now on she would be cool and dignified, part of the hardening process. Not one hint of emotion would be shown.

She didn't want coffee, and he could damn well make his own! She collected her small suitcase and handbag from just inside the kitchen door and wondered just what he'd meant by his 'under the circumstances', but she wouldn't have asked to save her life. She wouldn't allow him to think that she had any interest in what he said or did. And he must be truly desperate to get rid of her to have made that journey to collect the rest of her things in the middle of the night, and then get up at dawn to phone around for a mini-cab driver.

Well, he couldn't be half as desperate for her to get out of here as she was!

Taking herself and her belongings, she let herself out of the front door and stood under the porch, sheltering from the drizzle, waiting for the car, glad she had her chequebook with her because the trip to London would cost an arm and a leg.

Just another reason why she, who hated violence, would be happy to scratch his eyes out! If he'd had any kind of conscience he would have driven her back himself and saved her a small fortune. He had put her in this humiliating situation—unable to go back to his parents' home even to collect her things, let alone to wait until Mark was ready to return to town, because of what they would now perceive her to be: the guest of one of their sons creeping off to spend the night with the other! She simply couldn't face that.

So perhaps her traumatic encounter with Daniel Faber had achieved something that whatever life had thrown at her in the past had failed to do. It had hardened her up. Made the heart that had always been loving and giving, searching for love and acceptance, wanting to be needed, turn hard and cold, capable of wanting to do physical violence to another human being.

Time would tell. It certainly felt that way right at this moment.

She lifted her chin defiantly and stared at the neglected garden, and heard the sound of an approaching car just as the cottage door she had firmly closed was opened behind her.

Daniel. Freshly shaved and wearing a soft cashmere sweater the same steely grey as his eyes, his dark hair damp and flopping over his forehead.

'No need to wave me goodbye,' Annie snapped,

turning to watch for the approaching car because looking at him hurt. 'Might I suggest that, should we ever have the misfortune to meet again, we pretend we don't know each other, and don't want to, either?'

He ignored her, strode down the path to the crooked gate. And Annie was too amazed to take umbrage as she watched a gleaming Daimler stop behind Daniel's Jaguar and begin the tricky process of turning in the narrow lane, making use of the convenient break in the hedge in front of a field gateway.

The driver, she saw with a jolt of shock, wore a dark green chauffeur's cap and matching jacket. She followed Daniel on shaking legs. How could she afford the fare such an outfit—a chauffeur-driven class car at optimum Bank Holiday rates—would demand?

The short answer was, she couldn't. She thought of her dwindling bank account, her share of the bills back at the flat waiting to be settled, this month's salary not due to be paid in until next week, and shuddered. But no way would she plead poverty in front of Daniel Faber. No way would she humble herself.

Her chin in the air, her expression as blank as she could make it to hide the sick apprehension inside, she edged past the Jaguar and watched the chauffeur emerge from the Daimler—a short, rotund middle-aged man with a nice fatherly face. Maybe, if she explained her financial predicament once they were under way, she and the driver could work something out. If the company he worked for was fairly local— which certainly seemed logical considering the earliness of the hour—maybe he could be persuaded to drop her off at the nearest phone box. Then she could contact Mark, explain what had happened, and beg him to pick her up and drive her back to London.

It would mean making his long weekend a short one, but she'd been doing him a big favour in agreeing to come as his guest. And it was *his* hateful brother who had got her in this mess. So Mark owed her.

Daniel and the driver had exchanged a few words and both of them were smiling, almost as if sharing a joke. As she drew nearer the driver turned and looked at her, and his smile turned into a grin.

Had Daniel been saying something about her? Or was it simply the way she looked? Annie supposed she did present a humorous sight, her mane of long hair more wild and crinkly than usual, last night's party-wear shrunken and crumpled, the skirt showing more leg than even she was comfortable with, the sleeveless top all clingy and gaping at the deep V-neckline, displaying an interesting amount of cleavage. It might have embarrassed her, but she wasn't going to let it.

Her pace didn't falter as she approached the car, not looking at Daniel, smiling widely for the driver. She was right, he did look nice and fatherly, so it would be easy to explain her difficulties to him. He probably had daughters her age of his own, and would understand all about the kind of fixes a girl could get herself into.

'Miss Kincaid will give you her London address,' she heard Daniel saying as she handed the driver her suitcase. She didn't so much as glance his way. From this moment on, he didn't exist. It had to be so. To think about what had happened, the way he had made her feel, would be to torment herself viciously and needlessly.

While her suitcase was being stowed in the boot she let herself into the front passenger seat. Easier to talk informally here, rather than perched like royalty in the back. The driver's face was impassive as he slid in beside her and began to ease the stately vehicle down the track, so he obviously didn't mind her choice of seating position.

Annie sighed with deep relief. They were on their way and she could begin to put the whole emotional, humiliating experience behind her.

She gave breezy, non-committal replies to the driver's comments on the miserable state of the weather, his forecast that it would improve later in the day. She couldn't concentrate on anything while she could still see Daniel in the wing mirror, standing at the head of the steep track, his hands in the pockets of the dark narrow-fitting trousers he was wearing, staring after the receding car as if to make sure she was well and truly going.

But as soon as they turned onto the metalled road and Daniel Faber was lost to view she took her eyes from the wing mirror, wriggled down more comfortably in the leather-upholstered seat and gave her attention to the driver.

She had some bargaining to do.

As if sensing her eyes on him, the driver gave her a sideways glance. He looked curious and slightly amused, and again she wondered what Daniel had been saying to him. She gave him her big and beautiful smile and felt her face go pink, because she was beginning to be nervous about asking, feeling more than just a bit of a fool.

She tried to calm herself by breathing deeply, but it didn't help. It just made her breasts look as if they were trying to burst out of her scrumpled, shrunken top. She caught another sideways look and saw the driver's eyebrows shoot upwards, disappearing under the peak of his cap, and she knew it was now or never, because soon she'd get to feeling too nervous and embarrassed to say a thing about her precarious financial state and would find herself in London facing an enormous bill.

'Look—' she began breathlessly, then gathered herself and forged on, 'I can't afford to pay the fare, and I'm sure you'd like to get back in bed—the best place to be on a wet Bank Holiday weekend—so I've a proposition to put to you...' Her words died in her throat as, horrified, she watched a tide of scarlet cover the driver's face.

He thought she'd been propositioning him! Suggesting he waive the fare in return for bedtime favours! All she'd been doing was trying to cover her embarrassment by injecting a touch of humour, suggesting he go home, take it easy after dropping her at the nearest public phone box!

But the words had dried up in her throat with the sheer, excruciating awfulness of knowing what he was thinking, and before she could collect herself and correct his misconstruction he cleared his throat and said, 'That won't be necessary, miss. There is no fare to pay, as I'm sure you know. I work for Mr Faber, attached to the bank. I'm driving you back to London on Mr Faber's instructions, in the line of duty.'

And what could she say to that? Nothing. Annie just knew that if she tried to explain, to say anything at all, she would only come out with something to make things worse. If they could *be* any worse!

He obviously thought she was some cheap hooker! A dawn call from his boss, instructions to collect a female from his weekend hideaway and deliver her back to London—it would have certainly set him thinking.

Seeing her rumpled, dishevelled state—more than hinting at a night of debauchery—would have confirmed thoughts already pointing in that direction. A night bought and paid for, he would have decided, noting that his boss and the female didn't even say goodbye. A business arrangement.

He would have kept those thoughts firmly under his peaked cap until, as he believed, she'd tried to proposition him! Now he was a figure of total disapproval, mute, tight-featured, still red around the neck.

Just one more reason for her to hate and despise Daniel Faber, she fumed, trying to make herself as small as she possibly could in the passenger seat, feeling a blush spread all over her body. And she stayed that way, silent, humiliated and miserable, until the driver took her case from the boot of the car outside the tall terraced house in Earl's Court where she roomed with her best friend Cathy.

Riven with embarrassment, almost weeping with it now, she wondered whether she should try to explain, then decided against. For one thing she probably wouldn't be able to get the words out without bursting into tears of humiliation. And for another he wouldn't believe her.

He would believe whatever it was that Daniel had been saying to him, believe the evidence of his own eyes and ears. She wouldn't put herself through that, and, besides, she would never have to set eyes on the man or his wretched boss again.

So she contented herself with a mumble of thanks and scrambled into the house as fast as her shaky legs would carry her, thankful that Cathy was spending the weekend with her parents.

Letting herself in, she left her case in the converted cupboard that passed for a hallway and pushed through into the sitting room, glad of the solitude and silence. She needed it if she was to get her head together.

She could occupy herself physically by tidying up, she thought glumly, getting rid of the heaps of magazines, clothes waiting to be ironed, dog-eared recipe books or cluttery bargains she'd found in the flea market draped and dropped over the mismatched armchairs, occasional tables and whatnots. She owed it to her long-suffering flatmate.

First she needed food. She still felt shaky after the traumas of the last couple of days. But the phone rang and she felt infinitely worse when Daniel said tersely, 'I'm on my way.'

Background traffic noises told her he'd pulled into a lay-by to use his mobile. Where? Why? She didn't want to see him. Didn't want him to see her disgracefully messy flat. 'How did you get my number?' she gulped.

'From Mark, of course. And your address.' The harsh tone of his voice made it sound like a threat. Then, 'I told him we'd had a lovers' tiff,' he drawled.

Was that a sanitised version of what he'd actually said to his brother? The change to that hatefully mocking tone made it seem likely. Why was he hell-bent on making everyone see her in the worst possible light?

'Then you wasted your time,' she said as calmly as she could, grasping the receiver more tightly because her hand was shaking, the palm slippery with nervous sweat. 'I don't want to see you, and unless you want to apologise we have nothing to say to each other.'

'Not even on the subject of blackmail?' he asked drily, and Annie felt her knees buckle with shock. What new horror was he cooking up against her now!

'You're mad!' she accused thinly. She couldn't handle this. Couldn't handle him. He was far too threatening, too dangerous on every level she could think of. 'And don't bother knocking on my door,' she threw down the line at him, 'because I won't be here. I'm on my way out right now. And don't bother waiting around, either. I'll be out all night having fun—a commodity that's in short supply when you're around!'

She cut the connection and laid the receiver down on the table so he'd get the engaged signal if he tried to reach her again, then swallowed convulsively. Why the giddy blazes had she told him that? Her dizzy brain and flyaway tongue had just reinforced his low opinion of her. She seemed doomed to say and do all the wrong things around the wretched man!

CHAPTER FOUR

DANIEL tossed the mobile onto the vacant passenger seat and gripped the steering wheel, white-knuckled, scowling. The wrenching pain in his gut wasn't down to jealousy. Hell, no. It was disgust—plain and simple disgust.

Though he might have known the little minx would be spending the rest of the day out, the night on the tiles. She'd be trawling for new prospects now that it appeared he'd successfully queered her pitch with Mark, because women like her worked that way.

When he'd discovered her unsubtle attempt to get her own back he'd phoned Mark from the cottage and asked how he could get in touch with her, spinning a yarn about a passionate one-night stand, but apart from that, sticking to the truth.

'I got rid of her first thing—women like that don't go with the light of day. But she left some things behind me so I need to know how to return them.'

'Sure. Got a pen handy?'

To his relief, his brother had sounded more amused than riven with sibling jealousy, and Daniel had congratulated himself on having acted before any real damage had been done. After he'd written down the address and phone number he'd asked for, Mark had told him lightly, 'We both know why we're cynics where women in general are concerned, but Annie's no Lorna. Don't let the way she looks and dresses

74

fool you. There's a sweet kid under that sassy exterior and I'd hate to see her hurt.'

Which meant Annie Kincaid was a damn fine actor or Mark was as easily fooled as he ever had been.

Some 'sweet kid'!

A woman who would fling herself at her fiancé's boss, who would then dump the poor sucker and make a play for her own boss, then, even though she'd made enough progress to be taken home to meet the family, happily share her bed with someone else, was neither sweet nor a child!

But she'd spiked her own guns when she'd reminded him of his fictitious bride-to-be. Obviously she'd expected him to say he'd changed his mind about his fiancée, that it was *her* he wanted.

Her arch reminder that he was supposed to be engaged to someone else had backfired on her, bringing him to his senses, letting him grab the misunderstanding and hang onto it.

The episode had taught him an unpalatable truth. He couldn't trust himself around Annie Kincaid. He had always prided himself on his control, but for some reason he completely lost it within sight and sound of that bundle of sensuality, the chemical reaction she sparked off in him making his mind fly to marriage and babies and happy ever after.

That was why the word 'marry' had sprung so easily to his lips when she'd derided the paucity of his bachelor weekend retreat, annoying him—he who had no intention of marrying in the foreseeable future.

Her reminder of the Freudian slip had brought him back from the brink. He had no intention of demeaning himself by making love to a woman without a moral scruple in her body, not even to get her out of his brother's hair!

At least he appeared to have achieved that.

Like Lorna, Annie Kincaid had a gorgeous body and a beautiful face and the firm intention to use both to get as much wealth as she could lay her pretty hands on—intent on selling her body to the richest man who could be persuaded to offer her a wedding ring.

When he'd decided to act, take Annie away from Mark, he'd had misgivings. To Mark it would have seemed like history repeating itself, and he hadn't been sure whether he could bring himself to risk his relationship with his brother even to save him from making another disastrous mistake.

Five years ago, the shock discovery that he, Daniel, was all set to marry the woman who already wore *his* own ring, had almost finished Mark. Both brothers engaged to the same woman, Lorna Fox, had been a sickening experience. But they'd weathered it, come to terms with the little bitch's avaricious machinations, their brotherly relationship emerging all the stronger.

Daniel had only been completely sure of the rightness of his actions when his brother had seemed utterly unfazed on the phone this morning. He had accomplished what he had set out to do, and, if his mother was right in her assumptions, Mark had finally seen Enid for the lovely person she was.

Daniel refastened his seatbelt, started the engine and rejoined the flow of traffic heading for London. Just one thing left to do. Toss the frivolous feminine fripperies back in her face. Sneaking them into one of the drawers, she'd obviously hoped his—unknown to her—fictitious fiancée would find them. A way of getting her own back? Or had she had a spot of blackmail in mind?

He aimed to find out.

Frustrating to discover she wouldn't be home. And tomorrow he'd be tied up all day and well into the evening with the head of a Japanese consortium. But he could wait.

Annie was first into the office as usual on Tuesday morning. She preferred to beat the worst of the rush hour traffic, the crowds on public transport, and liked the empty room, the silence broken only by the occasional chattering of the fax machine.

Self-admittedly chaotic around the home, she was neatness and order personified in her professional life. She always used this quiet time to get everything sorted, ready for the day ahead, when the rest of the small staff, and Mark, arrived.

And this morning especially she needed this time to herself, to try to tame the jitters that squirmed through her blood and sent her brain into panic. She was going to have to explain about Saturday night and she wasn't looking forward to it at all.

She had no qualms about telling the truth, laying all the blame on Mark's horrible brother. After the way he'd treated her, Daniel deserved it. But would Mark believe her? Why should he believe her above his own flesh and blood? And why should that be so important?

Because she liked and respected her boss, enjoyed working for him, and she would hate to think of him looking at her and seeing a woman who would sneak away from a house-party to spend the night with a man she'd only just met, she answered herself.

Did the way she looked, the way she dressed, really lead people to think the worst of her, to think she was easy, anybody's? Until this last weekend she had never given it a thought, but she'd been brooding about it ever since she'd got back home. Had Aunt Tilly been right to smother her in shapeless brown gabardine and thick wool in winter and smothering bunchy cotton things in summer?

Annie sighed deeply and began to open the post, putting the letters for Mark's immediate attention neatly on his desk. This morning, knotted up with nerves over having to face Mark, she had borrowed one of her flatmate's crisply ironed white cotton shirts and put it on beneath her own plum-coloured suit— the soberest colour in her entire wardrobe.

But it had looked ridiculous poking out of the collarless deeply dipping neckline of the nip-waisted jacket with its flirty peplum that flared out above the short straight skirt.

So she'd taken it off again and here she was, wearing the type of clothes she enjoyed so much. And, apparently, looking like a trollop!

She felt a lump in her throat, as if she was about to cry, so told herself to grow up. She could dress how she pleased; she wasn't responsible for people's nasty minds. This was how she always looked around the office, and Mark had never once tried anything on with her, or said anything remotely out of place—and if he had she would have told him where to jump, not like his rotten older brother—

She bit off that thought immediately, knowing where it would lead. The way she had reacted around Daniel was bad enough; she didn't have to go over it inside her head and send herself crazy, and—

'Morning, Annie.' Mark breezed in on the dot of nine, grinning. Annie gave him a tweak of a smile and dipped her head quickly so that her hair tumbled wildly over her face, hiding it. From the outer office she could hear Sally, the secretary she shared with Mark, moving around, booting up the computer, setting up for a busy day ahead.

Annie swallowed convulsively. She had to do it now. Explain. The longer she put it off, the worse it would get. She could just imagine him looking at her and wondering why he had never before realised she had the morals of an alley cat.

'Mark—about the weekend. I really can't apologise enough. The party. It was unforgivable—' Her words tumbled over themselves in a mumbled rush; she couldn't get them out fast enough.

'An eye-opener,' he agreed, 'but hardly unforgivable. These things can happen, right out of the blue.' He was sitting behind his desk now, his elbows on the arms of his chair, his long fingers steepled in front of his mouth as if hiding a smile he couldn't wipe off. 'No need to make a song and dance about it.'

He was believing the line Daniel had intended him to believe. He didn't seem shocked, or angry because she had rudely left his parents' home without saying so much as goodbye and thank you for having me. So why didn't she simply leave it at that, put it all behind her and get on with her life?

Because she couldn't. Already the list of people

who thought badly of her was horrifyingly long.
Mark's parents, Enid, Daniel and the chauffeur. She
couldn't wait to strike Mark, at least, off that list and
hope to goodness he would convince his family of her
integrity.

And maybe her real, real reason for wanting to jus-
tify herself was the hope that Mark, in turn, would
come clean and explain to Daniel precisely why she'd
gone home with him last weekend.

She'd told Daniel that she and Mark weren't romantically involved with each other but he hadn't
even been listening to her. He had made up his mind
about her and that was that. She had known mere
words of hers wouldn't change his opinion.

Mark was the only person he would believe. Even
though she would never see Daniel again—unless he
carried out his threat to visit her home to discuss
blackmail, of all ridiculous things—she wanted him
to change his jaundiced view of her. It was desperately important to her, but she wasn't mentally up to
analysing why she felt so emotional about it.

'Please listen to me, Mark,' she begged, her big
eyes suspiciously bright. 'I first encountered your
brother at a party. I was still engaged to Rupert. We'd
had a row and, well, I thought I should try to make
things right again. I thought I saw him slip out onto
the terrace so I went after him, and kissed him. But
it wasn't Rupert—it was your brother. As soon as I
realised the mistake I headed for the hills.'

She felt her face go fiery red, more because of the
memory of how Daniel's kiss had affected her than
that deliberate untruth. 'Then, when he saw me again
at your parents' home, he thought what you meant

them all to think—that we were an item. For some reason he believed I'd behaved badly to Rupert, and he didn't want me around you. So he sort of hi-jacked me and made you all believe we'd run away for a night of lust.'

While she was speaking Annie wasn't sure if her boss was following her breathlessly emotional explanation of events, but guessed he must have because as soon as she paused to take in a much needed gulp of air his face suddenly sobered up and he nodded his head slowly, a slight frown pulling his brows together. He must have understood.

'And it wasn't a night of lust?' he asked, rising, beginning to pace the office floor, swinging round to meet her suddenly brimming eyes.

Annie couldn't answer. She'd already lied about leaping out of Daniel's arms the moment she'd realised her mistake. She'd done no such thing. She'd wanted the magic to go on for ever, and had only fled when things started to get out of hand and she'd come to her senses.

Her face went pink. She simply couldn't bring herself to lie again. She said, her voice quavering ominously, 'When you next see him, would you tell him? Tell him there's nothing between us? Tell him why I was at your parents' home?' She began to tremble and tears spiked her long dark lashes.

Mark gave a ragged sigh, took two paces over the floor and folded his arms comfortingly around her. 'Of course I will! Don't upset yourself this way.' He patted her back soothingly as she buried her face in his shirt and snuffled. 'His opinion of you matters a lot, doesn't it?' he asked astutely, and she didn't have to answer that, because he knew by her earlier evasion of his question that she and Daniel hadn't been playing Snakes and Ladders all through that night.

His voice took on a harder tone. 'If he's hurt you, sweetie, I'll—'

'You'll do what?' The dark drawl made the hairs on the back of Annie's neck stand up. He had no need to introduce himself.

'Dan!' Mark would have released her, turned around to face his brother as he closed the office door behind him, but Annie clung on for dear life, the shock of Daniel's appearance turning her legs to cotton wool.

Bad enough that he should have walked in unannounced. His finding her in Mark's arms was even worse. His humiliating opinion of her would be intensified.

It was.

Seeing them together, in each other's arms, sent a savage pain wrenching through his gut. Anger, he told himself, his knuckles white on the package he was carrying. Sheer, white-hot rage. Nothing else. Certainly not jealousy. No, of course not jealousy. Rot the thought!

He'd phoned his mother last night, well after Mark had left on the return journey to London. He'd apologised again for leaving the party, made his peace, fended off the loaded questions about Annie Kincaid. His mother didn't want to know!

Thankfully, she'd been easily deflected when he'd wanted to know how Mark and Enid had been getting along during the remainder of the weekend, since the last he'd heard his kid brother had finally seemed to have opened his eyes to the girl's existence as a desirable woman.

'I'm keeping my fingers crossed, but it seems to be going all the right way!' she'd said. 'They went for long walks and came back holding hands, and he took her out to dinner last night—that smart new restaurant on the Caper Cross road—and, so she tells me, he's invited her up to Town next week. He'll book her into a hotel—a show, then supper. He does appear to be serious. Oh, I do hope so! She's such a lovely girl.'

And so she was, Daniel thought darkly. If he could believe the evidence of his own eyes—and he could—too good for Mark!

After the Lorna débâcle the two of them had reacted differently. He, Daniel, had kept well clear of women, particularly those who were too gorgeously sexy for their own good—or his—channelling all his energies into his work, while Mark had gone to the other extreme, dating everything in short skirts, and rarely more than twice. Both had become hardened cynics when it came to the female of the species.

Had Mark decided to do what everyone wanted and settle down at last with the faithful Enid? Give his parents the grandchildren they kept saying they wanted while keeping Annie Kincaid as his bit on the side? Somehow Daniel couldn't believe that of his brother. At least, he was trying very hard not to.

His eyes narrowed as he watched Mark gently but firmly ease Annie away, patting her arms before he broke all physical contact. Look at it from a different angle, he told himself. Wasn't it more likely that when he'd walked in his brother had been in the process of breaking off his affair with his sexy PA—a combination of his belated interest in Enid and his belief that Amoral Annie had spent most of the weekend in his brother's bed!

Annie, however, had been clinging, turning on the tears, too, by the look of things. And he couldn't be one hundred per cent certain that Mark wouldn't fall for the little baggage's wiles. It would be a special type of man who could resist such a temptress.

She was rotten to the core, as Lorna had been, even propositioning poor old Barnes. His chauffeur, only this morning, had warned him, soft-voiced and obviously shocked down to his highly polished boots.

He had two reasons for his unprecedented appearance in his brother's office this morning. The first, business. He was taking a week off—a rare holiday—and Mark, if he was interested, could come along to meet a guy who could put a good business opportunity his way.

The second reason was his anger, his need to confront the devious, scheming trollop. If he couldn't pin her down at her home he'd do it at her place of work.

By planting that stuff in one of the drawers she'd wanted to make trouble for him, and now she was going to get it back, in spades!

She wasn't to know that his fiancée was fictitious. But now he had changed his mind. He was going to go for a different scenario entirely.

The long, tensely prickling silence was almost too much for Annie. She had felt Daniel's eyes on her the whole of the time, and when she'd risked a glance from around the curtain of her hair his eyes had bitten into her like lasers.

She knew Mark was aware of the tension, too, intrigued by it. One of his eyebrows was up near his hairline as he straightened his tie and ran a hand over his hair.

'So, what brings you here, Dan?' Mark asked, and Annie could have wept with relief. Someone, at last, had spoken. She couldn't have said a word to save her life.

'Part business, part pleasure.'

Astonishingly, Daniel Faber was smiling now, looking totally relaxed as he prowled further into the room, sitting on the edge of Mark's desk. Annie didn't trust him an inch. Why was he smiling, looking at her as if he was all ready to devour her, inch by slow and lingering inch?

He put the paper-wrapped package he'd been carrying down on the desk, tweaked it open and pulled out the oyster satin slithery nightdress she'd never wanted to set eyes on again. He held it up by the shoestring straps and said smokily, 'You left this behind, sweetheart. It looked so fantastic on you, I would hate to think of it getting permanently mislaid.' And he tossed it to her, his face transformed by that wicked, wicked smile.

Annie dropped it, the slithery silk slipping through her fingers, her reflexes slowed down to nil. Shock and embarrassment had made her mouth fall open, her eyes go wide and luminous. She couldn't understand this.

And then, as she saw the huge grin on Mark's face as he passed behind his brother to get to his leather swivel chair, she did. She understood it all. Daniel was doing everything he could to discredit her in her boss's eyes, making sure that whatever she said to exonerate herself she would never be believed!

Deeply, helplessly embarrassed, she retrieved the nightdress with shaky fingers, bunched it into a ball, and then heard the note of intimacy in her tormentor's voice as he asked, 'Would you make coffee, sweetheart, while I discuss a business proposition with your boss?'

She would go to Brazil to pick the beans if she could, and take a very long time coming back with them! Cringing, she fled from the room, dropped the hated nightwear in Sally's wastepaper basket and disappeared into the cubbyhole to put the kettle on for coffee.

'Hey! I could have done that,' Sally called out from the adjoining office. 'I'm supposed to be the dogsbody around here, not you!'

Annie pulled a face at the kettle. She'd thought Sally had been engrossed in her filing. She didn't want to talk right now. To anybody. She wished she could become invisible.

'Hey, did you see the guy who walked in? 'Course you did—silly me!' Sally was in the doorway now. 'What a hunk!' She rolled expressive brown eyes. 'And, boy, what a steaming temper!'

'Coffee?' Annie asked grittily. His temper had suffered an amazing sea change in the space of a few minutes. Only it was all a twisted act. He had smiled at her and 'sweethearted' her for his own devious ends, and she didn't want to talk about it. Or anything. She wished she'd never set eyes on him, wished he didn't exist. Wished she could wipe what she felt for him right out of her heart and mind.

She set two cups on a tray with cream and sugar, and another two, for her and Sally, on the worktop. Sally the unsquashable burbled, 'Oh, I do love that suit! I wish I could wear clothes like yours.' She grimaced at her cream-coloured blouse, her sober grey skirt. 'I just don't have the figure for it.'

Or she had more sense, Annie corrected sourly, vowing there and then to do the hitherto unthinkable—get all her hair cut off, right off, as near to her scalp as possible, and spend her next surplus money on something stodgy and brown, cut like the back of a bus.

Rupert had been right when he'd told her to tone down her act. Maybe she should look him up, tell him she had turned into the dedicated career woman he had wanted her to be, had given up on wanting a big rambly house filled with babies, had thrown away all her lovely, colourful, startling clothes.

Just thinking about it made her deeply depressed.

She poured the boiling water over the granules and handed the tray to Sally. 'Take it in to them, please, then we'll check through the paperwork for that shipment of fabrics from Asia.'

No way was she walking into that room again, not until Daniel was safely off the premises. And then she'd probably hand in her resignation! She would never be able to look Mark in the eye again!

Taking the two extra cups, she put them down on Sally's desk and drew up a chair. They'd get to work, and when Daniel left she'd pretend she couldn't see him, and then she'd see if she could find the courage to face Mark.

But she and Sally had been working for less than

five minutes when Mark buzzed through and asked her to get her butt back in his office.

Her insides felt like jelly as she reluctantly got to her feet. What had Daniel been saying to Mark? Going into all the gory details? She didn't think she could face them, Daniel in particular, not when he knew the shameful truth about her. Knew that although he had made his contempt for her crystal-clear he only had to touch her to make her body burn with the all-consuming flames of desire.

Yet she wasn't a complete wimp, she told herself as she tweaked the creases out of her skirt. She could ride out the storm of embarrassment. She could do anything she had to do.

'You wanted me?' she enquired of no one in particular as she stalked into Mark's office on her very high heels. And she saw sudden dark colour flood Daniel's unforgivably gorgeous, unforgettably male face.

Now what had she said? she wondered, then put the query out of her head as Mark, his hands crossed behind his neck, his feet propped up on the desk, told her, 'I've got a job for you. Tuscany—how does a week among the olive groves, sipping Chianti grab you?'

It did—oh, how it did! A week away was just what she needed to get over her traumatic long weekend—something else other than her rabid emotional response to Daniel Faber to concentrate on. 'Great!' she said quickly, refusing to look at her tormentor, who was still perched on the edge of the desk, watching her. 'So when do I go? And why and where to, exactly?'

She was already reaching for her notepad, thankful her passport was in order, looking forward to the project, whatever it was, when Mark drawled, 'You leave tomorrow,' snatching her breath away. He robbed her of it entirely when he went on, 'The accommodation's sorted. Dan has the use of a friend's converted farmhouse in the hills above Volterra—you'll be staying there with him. Apparently—' he swung his legs down off the desk '—there's a guy who creates wonderfully saleable alabaster stuff. Small sculptures, bowls, plates, ornamental columns—the sort of thing interior designers go crazy for. Dan will set up a meeting. He's happy to take time out from a well-earned holiday—the first I've known him take in years.'

He stood up and grinned at his brother. 'You take good care of my assistant, do you hear? She's a very special lady.'

Daniel got to his feet. 'Don't I know it!' He draped an arm casually around Annie's rigid-with-shock shoulders and dropped a kiss on the side of her frozen face. 'I'll pick you up from here, ten o'clock in the morning. Barnes will drive us to the airport.' His eyes burned into hers, the sensual curve of his mouth seemingly cruel now. 'I can promise you an extremely interesting trip, sweetheart.' And he walked from the room, his commanding male body elegantly packaged in dark, expensive tailoring, leaving Annie gasping for air.

'I can't go.' She sank into the nearest chair. She didn't know why Daniel was acting as if they were a loving couple when she knew he thought she was scum. She didn't know what he thought he was up to, only that it was no good. She wouldn't be a willing victim of his tricky, scheming brain!

'And why not?' Mark looked up from his neglected morning post, his eyes bland.

'It's too short notice. Anyway...' She gathered her excuses together, searching for the one that would convince him to go in her stead. 'You're the one who jets around the world, buying and selling. I get to stay home and mind the office. I don't know how to set up a deal.'

Her eyes challenged him to argue with that. He didn't, he simply said, 'Then it's time you learned. Besides, it was Dan who suggested you go.'

'And you have no say in it?' Annie couldn't believe she was hearing this. Did everyone jump when Daniel Faber told them to?

Mark lowered his brows at her. 'I think the world of my brother; I owe him everything. Five years ago I was working my socks off for another company in this line of business, and something happened to blow my world apart. He came to the rescue, bankrolled me, set me up on my own—which was the one thing that helped me get my head straight again. So if Dan wants something of me—which, I might tell you, he rarely does—then, yes, I'm only too happy to do anything I can to oblige.'

Annie stared at him, tongue-tied. Mark wouldn't believe her if she told him his sainted brother had horns and a forked tail. She could always hand in her resignation, right here and now, provided she could get her tongue to work. But then where would that leave her? Unemployed and in debt!

'Look...' Mark relaxed back in his chair, his tone

milder, almost sympathetic. 'I know something's going on between you two, so don't bother to deny it. Even if he hadn't returned your nightdress, made his interest in you very plain, a person would have to be blind and deaf and very possibly dead to miss the sparks that crackle around the pair of you when you're anywhere near each other!

'And I know you, too, Annie, don't forget. I know you're a sweet and generous soul, and really still fairly wet behind the ears. So I guess you're a bit confused and troubled by the suddenness of what's happened.

'My advice is, use the week in Tuscany to get to know each other better, consolidate your relationship. And before you ask, no, I didn't tell him about the real reason I wanted you to visit with me last weekend. You can sort that out yourself—part of the learning process over the next seven days.

'And don't worry. He'll treat you with kid gloves. When he first mentioned the trip and said it might be a good idea for you to get hands-on experience I agreed it made good business sense. But I remembered how agitated you were early on this morning and guessed you couldn't handle the suddenness of it all. So I told him that I'd let you go provided he backed off where you were concerned.

'He's not a monster, Annie. He's got the message and will give you the space you need to progress more slowly in this very new relationship. And believe me, Dan's the greatest. Despite that tough exterior, he wouldn't do a thing to harm a living soul.'

Annie got unsteadily to her feet. Mark was seeing his brother through rose-tinted glasses; he would never believe that his hero had a dark side. A side that had him calling a girl bad names then not being able to keep his hands off her. But she could point him in that direction!

'You're as bad as he is!' she snapped, standing rigidly straight, glad to have her backbone back. 'Tricky and devious. All smarmy words that mean nothing at all. It's all your fault, in any case—you got me into this mess in the first place, with your sneaky schemes to get that nice girl off your back!'

She paused to gulp in breath, ignoring his staring surprise. He looked as if a tame pussy cat had suddenly jumped up and started to savage him to death. 'You must know your precious Daniel is soon to be married—if he let scum like me into the secret he will certainly have confided in his tail-wagging little brother! Yet you condone what's ''going on'' between us, give him your blessing and think you can make it all right by telling him to be gentle with me— or whatever rubbish it was you told him! What do you think I am? No, don't answer that!'

Annie scooped up her handbag, her head held high, her eyes spitting outrage. 'I'll go on this trip because I need the experience. And not the sort of experience you and your wretched brother have in mind! But as soon as I land back in England I'll be looking for another job. So don't bother firing me! And now,' she ended on a note of sour triumph, 'I'm taking the rest of the day off to pack.'

Annie stalked out leaving her boss looking as if he'd been run over by a bus and had only just realised it.

CHAPTER FIVE

ANNIE waited while Daniel collected the hire car at Pisa airport, her head in the air, looking neither to right nor left, ignoring the unwelcome, openly admiring male looks that were being lobbed her way and the occasional remarks—luckily in Italian, so she couldn't understand what was being said.

She was holding herself together—not without difficulty.

Instead of packing yesterday, she'd given herself a good talking to, got her head straight, and fixed on a way to handle this week in Italy—with him. Cool, composed and businesslike. That was the way, the only way. She would ignore his insults, let him know that his opinion of her was a matter of supreme indifference, and if he tried to touch her she would slap him.

So her packing had been a last-minute rush, and she'd arrived at the office deliberately late—five minutes to the second after Daniel had said he would pick her up. No time for any conversation with Mark, just a few hasty instructions which she'd accepted in silence.

And where the heck had Daniel got to? She seemed to have been waiting for hours, not the few minutes he had mentioned.

Not that she wanted his company; she most certainly didn't. But she was stuck with it, and her curvy figure in the close-fitting white cotton jeans and amber silk camisole top she'd chosen to travel in was drawing too much male attention.

At least so far he hadn't given her cause for grief, she gingerly consoled herself. No insults, no touching. No replay of yesterday's astonishing endearments, big smiles and casual kisses. Polite, considerate behaviour throughout the journey. Only once, when they'd been waiting to board their flight, had she almost lost it.

'I'd like to book into a hotel when we reach Volterra,' she'd said as he'd handed her her first-class ticket. The thought of being holed up with him, somewhere in the hills, held no appeal whatsoever. Just look what had happened when they'd spent the night together in his cottage—they'd come within a whisper of making wild, passionate love!

She was fully and shamingly aware of the way he could make her lose every last one of her wits, draw forth responses from deep within her, responses she hadn't known she had to give until she had met up with him.

'Get real, Annie! This time of year every room in the town will be booked. You'll be quite—comfortable—with me.'

One corner of his mouth had turned down in the lop-sided half-smile she found so incredibly sexy. She'd had to look away. Quickly. That smile, coupled with the intense smoke-grey eyes threw her off balance.

She'd avoided looking at him again.

But now her eyes were searching for him, and the moment she saw his tall figure striding towards her her heart jerked with pleasure. No, not pleasure.

Relief. She'd started to think he'd abandoned her. And she needed him—if only to set up the meeting between her and the alabaster man!

But to her annoyance she couldn't stop smiling. She would not, repeat, *not*, let him think she was smiling at him. He would take it as a come-on! So when the youth whom she'd seen lurking for the last five minutes approached her, and said something incomprehensible in rapid Italian, she released that great big smile on him—got it out of the way, so that she was able to present a cool, indifferent mask to Daniel when he pushed himself firmly between her and the youth, took her arm and practically frog-marched her from the terminal.

'I can't trust you on your own for five minutes!' he snapped acidly, scowling at her answering look of incomprehension. He wanted to shake her until her dazzling white teeth fell out! She went out of her way to dress provocatively, flirt with strangers. It was doing his head in!

He'd taken far longer than necessary to collect the car, stow their luggage and drive round to Arrivals, deliberately giving himself time to decide whether or not he was doing the right thing.

He'd been surprised, prepared for a much longer battle when Mark had agreed to the Tuscany trip. Wearily unsurprised when his brother had told him in no uncertain terms to back off where Annie was concerned. He had hoped his brother would have had enough sense to write her off when, after last weekend's charade, he, Daniel, had made that unprecedented visit to his place of work and put on the act of his life—making like a lover with medium-term intentions.

It would seem as if the baggage had her hooks very firmly bedded in, that Mark was willing to forgive her sexual peccadillos, provided she made herself available for him.

His plan had seemed, at that point, doubly necessary. But this morning she'd barely said a word to Mark, looked at him as if she despised him. And on the flight out she'd seemed a changed woman—polite, totally in control. Quiet. Not one sign of the former provocative fire and fizzle, the open sexuality that very occasionally turned to a little-girl-lost vulnerability when she was startled or unsure of herself.

He'd got to the point of deciding his master plan was way over the top, that apart from setting up that meeting he'd avoid her as much as was possible during the coming week, until, going to collect her from where he'd asked her to wait, he'd seen that youth lever himself away from the column he'd been leaning on and strut towards her, saying something, grinning.

Something that had made her turn to him and give him a smile hot enough to melt his socks off his feet. It had made him want to punch the hapless young Italian straight in the eye!

So, as far as his master plan went, it was all systems go.

'Are we nearly there?' Annie asked, forced into breaking the hour-long silence, letting go her vow to be cool and composed whatever the aggravation. She simply couldn't stand it a moment longer.

He was a moody devil! The contrast between the stony-faced man in the driver's seat and the urbane, considerate travelling companion of the earlier part of the day was startling. And the way he'd grabbed her and practically dragged her out to the car had been the tactics of the caveman!

She saw the tensely held muscles loosen up beneath the soft white cotton of his short-sleeved shirt, as if he was consciously forcing himself to relax. And his voice was smooth, tinged with just enough warmth to thaw the atmosphere when he answered, 'Not long now. We skirt the town of Volterra and head up to the hills behind. We should be comfortable.' He turned briefly, his smile taking her breath away. 'These friends of mine, Bill and Josie Saunderson, make a point of spending at least two months out of every twelve at La Cascina. They bought the near derelict farmhouse for a song ten years ago, spent a great deal of money and effort on it. And although they're only in their early forties they're practically counting the days until they can retire there!'

'Fancy,' Annie murmured caustically, wondering why, apart from that episode at Pisa airport, when his behaviour had reverted to what she regarded as the norm when around her, and after his subsequent moody silence, he was being so darned nice.

'They don't believe in roughing it, so you won't have to put up with primitive plumbing and candle-light.' Again the glancing smile from smoke-grey eyes. 'Though I'm told candlelight can be romantic.'

Her heart skittered. He was flirting with her! Carrying on yesterday's Oscar-winning performance—and not for Mark's benefit, either.

Why?

Because he'd already decided she was anybody's so he might as well grab himself a slice of the action? Finish off what had started back at his cottage?

Not if she could help it!

But could she help it? Knowing how susceptible she was to the sheer power of his male magic, she wasn't too confident about her ability to resist. She would just have to keep reminding herself that he was the type of louse who would make love to another woman while his fiancée wasn't looking.

'No comment?' He glanced at her pale profile, the stubborn jut of her chin, and swallowed a mouthful of spiky rage. She was giving him the cold shoulder—with a vengeance!

The little minx could dazzle a perfect stranger with the fire of her smile but give *him* nothing but ice! Remembering the way she'd looked down her nose at his weekend cottage, he had to fight to control the urge for sarcasm as he told her, 'You won't be called on to do a share of the chores at La Cascina. We have the loan of the maid who looks after Bill and Josie when they're in residence.'

'Great,' she replied tightly, detecting a trace of irritation in his voice. Perhaps he'd get the message and realise she didn't want to make conversation, wanted nothing to do with him at all—was only here because if she could pull off a successful deal it would look good on her CV and would surely help when she went job-hunting. Maybe she'd apply to the company Mark had worked for before big brother had set him up on his own. Which would be poetic justice.

She turned her head in a deliberately excluding

movement and stared out of the window at her side. They had skirted the medieval town of Volterra, high on its impressive ridge, girdled by ancient defensive walls, and were winding through rugged hills with views into distant, hazy valleys and glimpses of the silver loops of a winding river.

And then, suddenly, they were there. The narrow road ended at the foot of a twisty path strewn with clumps of camomile leading up to the long, mellow stone farmhouse set in a terraced garden brimming with sprawling roses and scarlet poppies.

Below them the valley dropped away, patched with cultivated fields, the dark green of the chestnut woods, down where the river looped, the red roofs and stout walls of little farms, and the early September heat haze threading through it all like a gauzy purple scarf.

Annie was glad to be out of the car, and not just because she ached to stretch her legs. Sitting so close beside Daniel she'd felt claustrophobic, aware of each breath he took, the easy way those long strong hands held the wheel, the bitter-sweet memory of how those same hands had touched her, stroked her far too willing body, igniting fires she had never really believed in but which now, unfortunately, she was finding almost impossible to put out.

'Like it?' Daniel had taken their cases from the car and drew level with her as she climbed the twisty path. She was tempted to speak the truth, tell him that she thought the carefully renovated house looked lovely, the view simply glorious and the silence something she could easily get used to after the never-sleeping noise of London.

A temptation she avoided, because she knew that

staying cool and aloof was the only way she could handle the situation.

She ignored the question, speaking only when he'd pulled a key from a side pocket and opened the heavy old door. 'Is it possible to set up that meeting for tomorrow?'

She walked through into what appeared to be the main living area—deep window seats, comfortable sofas, a graceful rosewood desk with a glorious patina and lots of little drawers with pretty ormolu handles. Daniel followed, dropping the cases on the terracotta-tiled floor.

'Besides being extremely talented, Giovanni Roselli is a very busy man. We'll be lucky if he finds a slot for you this side of the weekend.' He pushed his hands into the beautifully styled trousers he was wearing and grinned at her. 'Shall we explore?'

He looked so at ease, so relaxed, with a lock of soft dark hair falling over his forehead. Her fingers ached to brush it away, to touch warm skin, to learn the hard contours of his face with the tips of her fingers. But it was the endearing look of almost boyish excitement in those deep and smoky eyes that really got to her, making her heart clench with longing, a yearning she had no business to feel.

She swallowed clumsily, reminded herself of what a louse he really was and said, a little too gruffly for her liking, 'You could try, couldn't you? To fix an early appointment, I mean. The sooner it's done, the sooner I can go—get out of your hair, leave you to enjoy your break.'

'And what if I want you in my hair?' he queried softly, his mouth curving as he hooded his eyes and let them drift down to her feet, then slowly back to fasten on the soft full breasts that pushed against the thin fabric of her top.

Annie dragged in a harsh breath. 'I don't care what you want,' she pushed back at him roughly. Dear heaven, the implicit invitation was hard to resist! 'I'm here on business, not to entertain you.'

'Pity!' he said, and, hearing the laughter in his voice, she walked blindly through the room, high heels making a panicky sound on the tiles, opened a door into the kitchen, aware that he was following, sharply attuned to every move he made.

Daniel followed, watching her. The sway of her hips drew him with an enticement impossible to ignore. The sexual chemistry was stronger than anything he'd ever experienced before. Looking back, he could honestly say that Lorna had never affected him in quite this way, with such intensity, such compulsion.

Carrying out his plan to seduce her, make her forget his brother once and for all, was going to be no hardship. In fact, he decided as he felt his body stir uncomfortably, it would be a necessity!

Leaning against the doorframe he watched her move around, inspecting the contents of the fridge, the well-stocked cupboards, the gleaming copper pans that hung—along with bunches of garlic, onions and dried herbs—from overhead racks.

She probably didn't know how to boil water. Her hair was fabulous. She probably thought the working utensils were the latest thing in designer decoration. Her body was the most beddable he had ever set eyes on. And her face alone would ensure she would never have to actually work in a kitchen, or stand at supermarket checkouts, worry about meeting bills or how to afford new shoes for her children.

She, like all the other Lornas of this world, was on the look-out for the best meal ticket she could find—platinum-plated, if at all possible.

He knew she was annoyed with him, and was amused by it. He'd queered her pitch with Mark, at least temporarily. She was going to have to work very hard to wriggle back into favour, convince him that the time she'd spent at the cottage had been 'just one of those things' and a terrible mistake. He wondered whether Mark had told her about his burgeoning interest in the faithful Enid. Whether that was responsible for her attitude to his brother earlier today. Had Mark—heaven forbid—given all his attention to Enid merely to pay Annie back for sloping away?

Was it only a matter of time before they got their wires uncrossed?

He, Daniel, was going to make sure she didn't want to, and that she, like Lorna had, five years ago, would see the elder brother as the better catch. From what he'd observed, what Mark had said, it was on the cards that he was already halfway to falling for a mercenary little gold-digger all over again.

It was up to Daniel to stop it happening. For his brother's sake he would forget all his principles and take her on, force Mark to see her for what she was, then tell her, Nice try, but go find another rich sucker, and stay away from me and mine. He could hack it.

It was only a matter of time.

Annie staked her claim to the first bedroom she came across. There were four of them, Daniel had told her, each with its own *en suite* bathroom. Hers overlooked the frontage of the house with its magnificent panoramic views. Decorated in cool shades of blues and greens, furnished with pretty antiques, it was both beautiful and tranquil.

She needed that. Tranquillity had been in short supply over the past few days. And, as Daniel seemed in no hurry to set up that meeting, this room would have to become her refuge. The tension whenever they were together was too much to bear.

Unpacking could only take up so much time, and she was wondering whether to have a shower, or laze around in the bath, when she was alerted by the sound of voices on the path outside. Company? It would certainly ease the situation.

Peeking through the window, she saw Daniel talking to an elderly man. The visitor, dressed in a dusty blue suit, had arrived by bicycle and was waving his hands around a lot. Obviously a local.

Company or not, a local could tell her if there was a bus service up here in the back of beyond, or give her the phone number of a taxi service. Then she could be independent, remove herself from Daniel's disturbing presence for great stretches of time.

She had reached the foot of the stairs when Daniel walked in through the main door, leaving it open to the warm, late afternoon air. He was carrying a basket covered with a white cloth and the visitor was already pedalling away down the track.

Her heart sank. So much for information. Then she brightened, remembering the maid. She would be able to tell her about possible means of transport.

'That was Assunta's—the maid's—grandfather,' Daniel said, walking through to the kitchen. Annie followed, wanting to find out when the maid would put in an appearance. 'Apparently the poor girl tripped over the cat this morning and broke her collarbone. So, obviously, she'll be unable to come in as usual. The old man couldn't stop apologising, but I told him not to worry, and to tell Assunta not to worry, either.' He put the basket down on the table, his rangy shoulders lifting in a shrug. 'I said we'd manage fine, but boiling an egg is about my limit of culinary expertise.'

He saw stark dismay in the purple depths of her fascinating eyes and told himself, That figures. She can't even do that—boil an egg. Probably eats out all the time at some poor bewitched guy's expense. 'Apparently she gave her grandad a list and sent him out for fresh provisions so we'd at least have the makings of a meal. Thoughtful of her.' He pulled the cloth from the basket. 'I'll see what I can do with this.'

'This' was a plump fresh chicken, a crusty loaf, crisp vegetables and salad stuffs. Annie swallowed her disappointment at Assunta's non-arrival in a rush of sympathy for her injury and the prospect of working with such lovely fresh ingredients.

She often cooked for herself and Cathy, but Cathy was always on one faddy diet or another, and Rupert, when they'd been a couple, had always insisted on sending out for something trendy.

'Leave it to me.' Annie ran her eyes over the comprehensive range of copper pans, selected one and lifted it down from the overhead rack.

'You can cook?' Daniel rocked back on his heels, hands in the pockets of his slim-fitting trousers, one brow raised disbelievingly. 'Be my guest, provided you don't give us food poisoning—I would have thought your talents lay in other directions. Exclusively.'

Annie ignored him. She couldn't be bothered to fend off his insults. She was getting used to them, and his warped opinion of her morals, and besides, she was already assembling ingredients in her head.

As she'd noted on her earlier root around the kitchen, the fridge was stocked with fresh dairy produce, the cupboards with every tinned and dried food imaginable.

'Food poisoning? Now that's a neat idea—don't tempt me!' She gathered everything she needed, found a chopping block and a long sharp knife then expertly jointed and skinned the chicken, washed some mushrooms, sliced an onion, chopped garlic, popped the pan on the stove and drizzled in some olive oil.

'You certainly look as if you know what you're doing.' He had been watching her every move, unwillingly fascinated as usual. He could, he realised with a decided shock, spend the rest of his life watching her and never tire of the experience. Testosterone had a lot to answer for, he thought wryly.

'So?' she huffed defensively, then added crisply, 'Make yourself useful. See if you can find any dry vermouth—failing that, white wine would do almost as well.'

She was turning the chicken joints in the sizzling oil, and Daniel grinned at the bossy note in her voice, went to do as he was told and came back carrying two bottles, two glasses.

The crisply browned chicken pieces were now in a deep casserole with the mushrooms and onions, he noted, with the upward drift of one brow. He hovered, nose twitching appreciatively, as she added the contents of a tin of tomatoes to the copper pan and sprinkled dried herbs over the bubbling sauce.

'Smells good, at least.' But time would tell. The proof of the pudding...

When he'd first returned with the bottles she'd seemed totally relaxed, engrossed in what she was doing. Now, standing slightly behind her, close, he saw her slender shoulders go rigid. The instinct to reach out, massage the kinks out of those taut muscles, was pretty damn close to overwhelming.

He moved away. Touch her once and it wouldn't stop there. As he knew from past, brain-imprinting experience.

Yet the whole idea of getting her here instead of Mark, as had been his original intention, had been to seduce her away from his brother, keeping him safely out of her clutches. So why not begin right now? What was holding him back? Sometimes he believed that since meeting her she was sending him off his trolley, muddling his normally incisive mind, making him question his own motives.

He unscrewed the cap of the vermouth bottle and handed it to her. It wasn't that he didn't want to feel that gorgeous, unbelievably responsive body against his again. He did. The wanting had been a savage ache for days. And nights. It was just...

Just what?

Just that he felt, in some obscure way, that he needed to know her better. Delve into her psyche.

Reinforce his belief that she would deserve everything she got. Besides, their near miss back at his weekend cottage had been surrounded by anger. An angry sexual encounter wouldn't bind her to him long enough to see Mark safely off the hook. They would need to continue to see each other for quite a time after they returned to England for his scheme to work out the way he wanted it to.

Daniel uncorked the wine and filled two glasses just as Annie bent over to slide the prepared casserole in the oven. Her rear view, in those tight-fitting white jeans, made his throat clench.

He cleared the constriction roughly. 'You deserve a drink after all that effort.' He held a glass out to her, careful not to let his fingers brush against hers as she took it from him. He picked up his own glass and the opened bottle. 'There's a pleasant view out at the back, and a place to sit. Shall we?'

As he led the way through another door that led from the kitchen Annie followed, by way of an airy, whitewashed stone utility room complete with washing machine and deep freeze, racks of wine and more bunches of dried herbs.

Well, why not? She was heartily tired of being tense and on guard. Doing one of the things she enjoyed most—preparing a meal with first-class ingredients—had released something in her. It would be nice to sit in the early evening sun, sip wine and gaze at a slice of a country that was entirely new to her.

A thick oak door at the far end of the room gave on to a short flight of stone steps leading down to a flagged terrace. At one end was a padded swing seat with a shady awning, and at the other an ornate cast-iron table and chairs.

Daniel led the way to the table and Annie sat, sipped her wine thirstily. 'This is nice,' she said, and meant it. She decided the cooking session had been therapeutic, very, because she suddenly felt relaxed—even, strangely, in holiday mood, and she gave him her huge smile. And saw him blink.

He sat beside her, angled slightly in his chair so that he could see her as well as the sweeping vista of rumpled hills and deep valleys, terraced cultivation, gnarled old almond trees and the deeper green of olives, all drowsing peacefully under the slanting, rosy rays of the lowering sun.

'The view's entrancing,' Annie said after another deep swallow of wine, recalling, perhaps too late, that she'd been far too uptight to eat on the plane and that the alcohol would go straight to her head.

'It is from where I'm sitting.' His voice was slow, honeyed, and it told her what she didn't need to turn her head to discover. He wasn't looking at the view. He was looking at her.

Something sharp and sweet and tight twisted deep inside her. To banish it she would have made an excuse to go and check on supper, but as if to put her at her ease, make space, he asked lightly, 'Have you done much travelling, Annie?'

She huffed out her breath in relief. No need to scurry back to the kitchen after all. 'None. But I'd like to. I've always dreamed about seeing new places, different lifestyles.'

'Then why haven't you?'

'Lack of funds,' she answered openly, cheerfully.

He had refilled her glass, she noted, twisting the stem between her fingers, and decided to leave it to drink with supper. Already she felt rather too relaxed. Around Daniel Faber that wasn't altogether wise.

But, amazingly, she was enjoying chatting with him—no barbs, no insults, no need to counter-attack. 'Aunt Tilly was comparatively wealthy, but when she died she left everything to the church. I think she thought she'd done more than enough for me. I'm not complaining,' she told him earnestly, in case he thought she was. 'It was hers to do with as she pleased. So I had to make my own way—the same as the majority of the population. But it meant I don't have money to splash around on foreign holidays.'

Only on loads of gorgeous clothes, a little voice reminded her inside her head. But that had been her choice, although perhaps not a sensible one.

'You were brought up by an aunt?' he asked, his head tipped slightly on one side, his eyes narrowed against the low rays of the evening sun.

'There wasn't anyone else.'

'Tell me about it,' he said quickly, inexplicably needing to get to know as much about her as he could.

Annie shrugged, her lovely face sobering. Even now, after all these years, she still felt the loss. She rarely talked about it, and certainly not in any depth, but for some unknown reason she suddenly found she wanted to bare her soul to him.

'My parents were killed in a road accident. Dad had taken a day off work to go with Mum to choose a gift. For me. It was the day before my tenth birthday. It still haunts me,' she said quietly, her fingers tightening around the glass. 'I felt it was all my fault, though rationally I now know it wasn't.' She had never spoken about those earlier feelings of guilt to another living soul. Talking openly to Daniel was a welcome and totally unexpected catharsis.

'I was at school when I was told. What happened after is a bit of a blur. Somebody—police or the social services—' again the slight shrug '—took me to the only relative I had. Dad's much older sister, Aunt Tilly. She took me in out of duty. The poor thing didn't want me—I guess she didn't know how to handle me. She'd never married, never had a job, just been a dutiful daughter and stayed home, caring for my grandparents.

'I don't really remember them; they died within months of each other and Aunt Tilly inherited everything—house, shares, the lot. Dad didn't care about that, I know he didn't, but my aunt must have believed he did, because she was always justifying it, telling me she had been left comfortably provided for because she had done her duty. She was very strong on duty.'

'It must have been tough for you,' Daniel said softly, and she raised her eyes to him and saw compassion. It made her throat hurt. She lifted her glass shakily and drank to ease away the pressure, then he asked, 'Your father's estate—surely it came to you?'

She nodded. 'In a trust, for my upbringing. There wasn't much. Dad's job didn't pay well, and the house we lived in was rented, and I guess he'd never got around to taking out life insurance. Aunt Tilly said he had no foresight. She said I showed all the signs of taking after him in that respect, that I must be taught differently.'

'She sounds like a regular harridan,' he said gruffly, but Annie shook her head.

'She was doing what she thought best. She didn't want me, remember, and she couldn't love me, but she was determined to bring me up properly.' She gave him a weak smile. 'I guess I do have a tendency to leap first and think later. I think she felt it had to be beaten out of me.'

'Not physically, I hope!' Daniel sounded angry.

'No. There are other ways,' she answered tiredly, remembering the countless times she'd been sent to her bedroom, to sit for hour after boring hour in the bleak, comfortless, painfully tidy room to consider her sins. To learn gratitude, patience, humility—or whatever her aunt had felt to be lacking in her at that particular moment.

'Do you always turn the other cheek, Annie?' he probed, remembering her defence of her obviously cold and unloving aunt's behaviour.

She pursed her full lips, regarding him solemnly, her head tipped slightly to one side. 'When you're desperate for love you tend to overlook lots of things in the hope of earning it. Anyway—' she forced a perky note to her voice '—it's too nice an evening to remember miseries! I guess I should check on that casserole; it should be almost ready to serve. And I must make a salad.'

She stood up, her legs feeling as tottery as her smile. Too much emotion, she guessed. Too much wine. Food would help.

'I'll give you a hand.' Daniel followed her, his eyes thoughtful. 'After we've eaten, we'll talk some more.'

Talking had not been what he'd had in mind for

the remainder of the evening. But suddenly everything was changing, his perceptions were shifting, and his need to get to know her, really know her, was imperative.

CHAPTER SIX

'THAT was superb!' Daniel had had two helpings from the casserole, polished off most of the salad and most of the bread. He laid his cutlery down, offered her more wine and, when she shook her head, confessed, 'I thought you wouldn't know how to boil water.'

'Did you now!' She couldn't take umbrage; quite suddenly she felt far too relaxed. Good food had sobered her up, leaving her feeling mellow. And good conversation—nothing contentious, simply exploring each other mentally, discovering they had many tastes in common, deliberately not mentioning Mark, or her job, or the rest of his family, or what had happened between them in the past. Keeping to safe ground. Annie was making the most of it, knowing it couldn't last.

The slight evening breeze touched her skin like warm silk and a million stars were coming awake in the darkening sky. His teeth gleamed in his shadowed face when he smiled at her.

'Do you ever regret breaking your engagement to young Glover?' he asked. 'On the face of it I would have thought he was ideal husband material—a secure job, good prospects, all his own teeth and a full head of hair.' He gave her a small wry smile, then told her, 'It knocked him for six. It was months before he got his act together after you dropped him.'

There was no outward censure in his voice, but she

knew it was there, lurking behind the bland tone. He was Rupert's employer, and naturally he'd take his side. But she couldn't deal with that right now—she didn't want another fight on her hands and she was genuinely concerned by what he'd said.

'I had no idea,' she said thinly, hating to think she was responsible for hurting someone badly. But they would both have ended up miserable if the marriage had gone ahead. It wouldn't have stood a chance, not after Rupert had metamorphosed into Aunt Tilly. 'I thought he'd be relieved, not having to marry some-one like me.'

Relieved? Daniel caught the word and turned it over in his head. Any man who'd put a ring on her finger would go stir crazy if she took it off and gave it back! And as for the rest of her statement—

'Someone like you?' he queried. 'A highly sexed little minx who can't help hurling herself at strangers, kissing them until they forget everything and every-one?'

He regretted having to fracture the soft after-dinner atmosphere, the undreamt-of feeling of companion-ship that was beginning to feel like closeness, but it had to be said. He had to know. By the light of the stars he saw her face go tight, welcomed the outrage in her voice with a thoroughness that surprised him.

'No! Of course not! What the hell do you take me for?' She got unevenly to her feet, bumping against the table, hating him now for spoiling everything, for making her forget all the former hurtful insults, his terrible high-handed behaviour, the humiliation he'd heaped all over her, and then bringing it all back in barrow-loads with a few well-chosen words.

He rose quickly, gracefully, easily aborting her intention to stamp off to bed. He held her by her upper arms, that elegantly powerful body a mere fraction of an inch away from hers.

'Then tell me what you did mean.' His voice was soft, but it didn't lack insistence.

Annie shuddered, the closeness of him mesmerising her. She flicked the tip of her tongue over her lips and strove to combat the effect he had on her. 'I meant,' she began raggedly, 'that I wasn't, and never could be, the woman he really wanted. He kept trying to change me into someone else.'

His fingers tightened on her arms and his voice alone was a punishment as he bit out, 'You mean someone respectable?' He could understand young Glover trying. She must have driven the poor guy out of his mind.

'I suppose so, yes.' She confirmed it, then rocked him back on his heels as she added, 'He wanted me to cut my hair and have the crinkles straightened out. And to dress discreetly. And, well, I suppose I could, at a pinch, have done all that, to please him—if that was what he really wanted. But the rest was too much. We wanted completely different things. He wanted me to be a full-time career woman; he didn't want the expense or responsibility of children.'

'And you did?' With the tip of one finger he lifted her chin, exposing her face to what starlight there was. Something inside him was shaking. Had he got it all wrong? All of it? No, he couldn't believe that.

'Oh, yes. Lots of them. And dogs and cats and a big rambly country house to put them all in.'

Her smile was so beautiful, so wistful, it made him

close his eyes on a silent groan. Her simple words, the yearning behind them, had touched that hidden chord inside him. The first time he'd seen her he'd instinctively thought of a nursery full of babies, her babies and his, and nights of steamy passion. Their passion.

He dropped his hands, stepped back. That line of thinking would get him precisely nowhere.

Then, as if sensing his mood of harsh withdrawal, she said tentatively, 'Rupert—we'd have made each other very unhappy, so it was right to end it. But—but is he all right now? Did he get his promotion? He wanted it so badly.'

'Yes. To both. Plus, he's started seeing someone else,' he told her coolly, firmly back in control. She was making herself sound like Goody-Two-Shoes, and it didn't fit. 'If you're so all-fired perfect, tell me why you kissed me as if you couldn't get enough of it while you were still engaged to Glover? What did you hope to achieve? Or did Glover put you up to it, hoping to sway my decision over the promotion he "wanted so badly" his way?'

'Of course not!' she refuted hotly, stung by his impossible to follow changes of mood. She sighed. He was determined to make life difficult, to think badly of her. 'We'd quarrelled the day before that party and were barely on speaking terms. I saw him go out onto the terrace—at least at the time I thought it was him. I thought it was time we made up, tried to iron things out. That's why I kissed him. You. It was a mistake.'

The truth? he wondered. There was one way to find out. It all depended on how she answered his next question.

But she was talking, the stubborn line of her mouth so touchingly beautiful, making him want to take her in his arms and kiss her senseless. 'And while we're discussing my supposed sins—which, according to you, are both terrible and legion—I went to your parents' home as Mark's guest because he begged me to. He thought everyone would believe we were an item and stop pushing Enid under his nose at every opportunity. I wasn't too thrilled about it.' Her eyes snapped purple scorn at him. 'But, aside from liking Mark, and sympathising with him, I'm happy to do anyone a good turn if I can. And you can believe it or not. I don't care any more!'

But she did care; he knew that. Why else would her luscious lower lip tremble now, the thick, dark sweep of her lashes drift down to hide the sudden glitter of tears in her eyes? She cared, or she was a highly accomplished actor.

He dragged in a harsh breath, fighting his instincts. That little-girl-lost vulnerability made his raw desire to take her in his arms, hold her close and comfort her difficult to contain.

What she had said, touching on that weekend, had a ring of truth. It made sense—it was the type of thing his brother would do. He had always rebelled when people tried to edge him down a path he didn't want to travel. And Daniel had wondered why Mark hadn't punched him in the eye for stealing his woman. He'd cynically put it down to the fact that his brother had turned a blind eye, that one time, because he knew Annie Kincaid's failings but was too besotted to forget her.

Hellfire! He didn't know what he thought any

more! He asked the belated question that he hoped would prove something, at least. 'When did you realise you weren't kissing Rupert?'

She shuffled her bare feet. She'd kicked her high-heeled strappy sandals off ages ago. They were somewhere under the table. How to answer? She felt her heart flutter. Telling him the truth would make him think even more badly of her—if that were possible. But she knew she was already more than halfway in love with the impossible man, and she couldn't lie to him.

'As soon as you started kissing me back,' she muttered, feeling her face go scarlet, relieved it was too dark for him to see how much her confession was costing her.

She waited for the cold explosion of scorn, the inevitable insult. It didn't happen.

He said softly, 'Which was almost immediately. So why did it take so long for you to call a halt?' The silver gleam of his eyes pierced her through the growing darkness. He moved fractionally closer. The breath in Annie's lungs turned to lead.

'Because I didn't want it to stop. It was magic. No man, ever, had made me feel that way before,' she answered courageously, gathering her defences to fight the consequences.

He knew now. Knew what he did to her. He would take her admission as an invitation. A highly sexed man, he needed very little encouragement—as she knew to her cost. He would move in now, take up that invitation, forgetting about his out-of-sight future wife.

She thought about the unknown woman and shuddered for her. Vowed she wouldn't let it happen and waited, stiff-shouldered, to repulse his determined male advances.

They didn't happen, either.

Just silence. Long, stretching aeons of aching silence. The dark night wrapped around them, seeming to bind them in a world of their own. The breeze feathered her skin. She shivered, and pushed her way out of the spell the night and the man were creating. She turned and walked into the house, and heard him call softly, 'Goodnight, Annie. Sleep well.'

Physical tiredness and emotional exhaustion ensured she fell asleep quickly but woke frequently, tossing and turning until the light bedclothes resembled a battlefield in a fabric factory.

Moonlight filled the room, flooding through the gauzy curtains. Annie got up and closed the louvred shutters, her body burning beneath the filmy silk-chiffon nightdress she wore.

Burning for him, yearning for the man who slept peacefully on, under the same roof, knowing now, because she had as good as told him, what she felt for him. Not caring.

She should be relieved that her feelings were not important to him one way or the other. Relieved, she told herself, not edgy, frustrated, utterly miserable. She picked her brush up from the dressing table and pulled it through the tangled mane of her hair, beginning the regulation one hundred strokes. On the very rare occasions when sleep had eluded her in the past, this had always helped.

Not tonight, though.

The thirty-fifth stroke had her remembering his earlier words, when he'd accused her of being a sexy minx who threw herself at strangers, kissing them until they forgot everyone and everything. He'd meant himself. Her kisses had made him forget he was promised to another woman. He did want her. He *did*!

The fifty-sixth stroke had her acknowledging that she had to respect him for refusing to accept the invitation he would have taken her confession to be. Unlike that first wild embrace last December, or the emotionally fraught, passionate coming together at his cottage only last weekend, he had remembered the woman who wore his ring and had declined.

Which brought her to brush-stroke number eighty-one and the savage feeling of not wanting to respect him at all! It only, heaven help her, made her love him more!

On the final stroke she had to fight to stop herself from crying like the stupid baby she was. She had fallen in love and it was hopeless. So he wanted her. So that was no big deal. Anyone could get over a fit of lust. He had so obviously managed to.

Pity a person couldn't shake off love as easily. Because even if he hadn't picked out his future wife—which, God help her, she was inclined to forget at times—he would never be interested, long-term, in someone like her. He would only let a woman into his privileged life if she was 'respectable'.

He had as good as told her he thought she wasn't!

Contrary to Annie's beliefs, Daniel wasn't sleeping. He was leaning against the stone balustrading that separated the terrace from the sloping wild gardens, watching the pinpricks of light from the scattered farmsteads in the valley go out, one by shining one.

Trying to get the knots out of his brain.

Right. Think about it, he told himself crabbily. Use your brain. He lifted the glass held loosely in one hand and swallowed the last of the wine, wondered whether to open another bottle, and walked inside to the kitchen to make coffee instead.

Her confession that their wild embrace last December had been something monumental for her—as well as for him, did she but know it—had touched him deeply on more than one level. She had passed the test, told the truth.

Had she tried to make him believe she had thought Rupert was kissing her, feverishly caressing her wildly responsive body for the whole of those ten or so earth-shattering minutes, he would have taken her for a cowardly liar. The old saying about cats all looking alike in the dark simply didn't hold water.

But she hadn't lied. She'd opened up to him. Told him that no one else had ever made her feel like that. And that went for him, too.

So why hadn't he reached out to touch her? One touch was all it took, as previous encounters had demonstrated all too graphically.

He took a mouthful of scalding coffee and grimaced. He knew why. This was a whole new ball game. He had brought her here with one objective in mind; to make love to her until all thoughts of his brother flew out of her mind and she latched onto him like the little gold-digger he had thought she was.

But in that one important area she had told the truth. So the odds were on her telling the truth about everything else: her reasons for breaking her engagement to Rupert, her reasons for appearing with Mark at last weekend's house party—and as for what Barnes, his chauffeur, had told him, well, he'd discount that, put it down to wishful thinking. He could understand that. He'd done quite a bit of it himself around Annie Kincaid.

So, if he'd been wrong about her all along the line, then making love to her was out. Unless his intentions were serious.

He worried at the thought, his scowl monumental as he let hot water gush into the bowl and began on the stack of washing up.

Was he serious about Annie? He didn't know. He knew he wanted her. Like hell.

Abandoning the train of thought that seemed to be going nowhere, he tackled another—one that had only just occurred to him, one he skirted gingerly around while he scoured out the casserole. Then, sick of skittering around, he tackled it head on.

Why had he, who was—he believed justly—proud of his logical mind, done what he had done? Kidnapped her from his mother's birthday party, phoned back home to give everyone the impression that she was willing and eager to spend the night with him, made sure he got her out here with him. Anyone with even half a brain—less than half a brain—would have taken Mark quietly to one side, confessed his suspicions about Annie Kincaid's integrity—and explained why he had them—and asked for the truth about his brother's relationship with the sexy little minx, warned him off.

But, no, he'd gone ahead and done what in any

other circumstances would have been unthinkable. He'd forgotten he'd got a brain at all and acted on blind, unthinking instinct.

He hadn't even got the excuse of being fifteen years old and stupid with it!

The burning question was, Why? The answer came with blistering clarity.

He wanted her for himself. All to himself.

'Oh, isn't this lovely!' Daniel had driven them to the nearest village for fresh provisions. It was market day and the little square was overflowing with colourful, tempting stalls.

She'd been quiet and withdrawn ever since he'd come down at seven this morning to find her making breakfast in the kitchen, thanking him stiltedly for cleaning up last night's dishes but saying little else.

Her exclamation of delight as they'd come across the market was the first uninhibited comment he'd had from her. He found himself savouring it—and her stunning smile.

'Shall I?' She dipped her head in the direction of the crowded stalls and he grinned back at her, fishing a handful of lire notes from the back pocket of his jeans and putting them in her hand. Closing her fingers around the paper money gave him the opportunity he'd been looking for all morning. The opportunity to touch her without appearing to demand more. Feeling the warm skin beneath his, the slender, fragile bones, was every bit as good as he knew it would be. But it left him wanting so much more.

'Go ahead. There's a café right here,' he said thickly, nodding to the groups of tables on the pavement, shaded by brightly coloured umbrellas. 'I'll have a coffee waiting for you when you've finished.'

She looked adorable, good enough to eat. Her bright hair shimmering in the sunlight, her face lit with a kind of inner radiance, her gorgeous body clothed in narrow-fitting scarlet trousers and a matching sleeveless waistcoat.

He watched her bounce happily away on her ridiculously high heels—scarlet—what else?—to match her outfit—and melt into the crowds. And suddenly he was swamped by a wave of protectiveness the like of which he had never once experienced before. Something to do with what she'd told him about her growing up years. Repressed and unloved from the age of ten, she'd been looking for the love she'd missed out on.

He didn't need to search his memory banks for what she'd said last night, it was burned into his brain. 'When you're desperate for love you tend to overlook lots of things...'

She shouldn't damn well have to!

But he didn't know if it was all an act. Could he believe her? Or not?

By the time she'd finished shopping and found Daniel at his pavement table Annie was flushed and happy. Despite knowing no word of Italian—except for *grazie*, which she had used often, shopping had been a fantastic experience.

The stallholders were all so friendly, and just looking at the glossy piles of tomatoes, peppers and aubergines, the newly washed eggs and beautiful fruits, had been as good as visiting an art gallery. And if the experience hadn't made her forget last night's restlessness and the miseries inside herself, it had at least pushed them right to the back of her mind.

'I bought all sorts—I couldn't resist!' She put her carriers on the table, and the change. 'Fish for supper. I'll poach it in white wine with rosemary and thyme.' She sat, pushing her rioting hair back off her face as he signalled the waiter for fresh coffee. 'And a simply gorgeous-looking pizza we can snack on for lunch. I hope you like pizza?' Suddenly she looked unsure of herself, as if she'd done something out of place. Then she brightened, smiling at him as she lifted her cup towards her lips. 'Of course you must, especially as it's the real McCoy—not one of those cardboardy things you buy frozen in supermarkets back home!'

Daniel couldn't bear to look at her. The physical need to make love to her, brand her as his possession, was fast becoming uncontrollable.

He stood up, leaving the notes and the coins on the table for the waiter. 'Time to go,' he said tightly, afraid of the near desperate urge to take her here and now. He picked up the carriers and headed back the way they'd come, leaving her to follow. 'We'll call in at the wine merchants on the way back to the car,' he told her when she caught up with him, his voice oddly strained. 'Then head for home.'

'Home'. Wouldn't it be nice if it was? she mused, as she unpacked the shopping bags on the kitchen table, putting his restraint down to those rapid mood changes of his.

Her home, and Daniel's. But she mustn't let herself think like that. Fantasies and daydreams—even if you did recognise them as being just that—could only lead to more misery.

'I've just phoned Giovanni Roselli.' Daniel appeared in the doorway, leant against it and looked at her from lazily veiled eyes. 'We're meeting with him tomorrow—Friday. You'll then have the weekend to decide what, if anything, you want to handle, and we'll see him again on Monday to take the business further, if that's what you decide. OK?'

'Fine, thank you. It fits in perfectly with my flight back on Tuesday.' She was no longer as anxious as she had been to get away. Last night's discussion seemed to have cleared the air, for him, at least. He couldn't have been nicer or more considerate this morning, apart from that brooding silence when they'd left the square. And he'd actually stayed up last night to clear the mountain of dishes she'd left all over the place.

So the need to get away no longer seemed imperative. Since she could never be anything other than his friend, she wanted to hang around to savour the experience. Which was probably foolish, she decided. Foolish to torment herself, give in to the desire to be near him.

But she was foolish by nature—hadn't Aunt Tilly told her so often enough?

Daniel walked further into the room and Annie's heart performed a wild somersault. Soft, worn old denims, topped by a faded olive-green T-shirt, made him look not only long and lithe and utterly fantastic, but less formidable, more approachable. As if she could go to him, lay her hands against the taut muscles of his wide chest and tell him how much she loved him, wanted him, and he would understand.

Foolish she might be, but not *that* foolish! she told herself, firmly squashing the crazy impulse.

'Did you bring any sensible shoes with you?' he asked, idly inspecting the pizza she'd put out on an earthenware platter.

'Don't you like high heels?' Annie asked, sticking out one foot, hiking up the narrow hem of her trousers, her head consideringly on one side. She voiced her growing secret fear, 'Do you think they make me look tarty?'

Daniel's mouth twitched, his heart tightening. Displaying the delicacy of her high-arched foot and slender ankle in that strappy nonsense was not, as he would have arbitrarily decided twenty-four hours ago, deliberately provocative behaviour.

It was just Annie—wondering, asking a question, wanting an opinion. Because for some reason—probably all down to that old harridan of an aunt of hers—she didn't have a lot of confidence in the choices she made, because those choices went against everything she'd been brought up to believe. Annie, he suddenly knew, had very little idea of the effect she had on the members of his sex.

'Tarty? Never!' He smiled thinly at her. 'Elegant. Just right for what you're wearing.' He played it down as much as he could, for his own sake. He was beginning to have a sneaking suspicion that the now mountainous lust he felt around her was responsible for making him see her in a new light, a way of making what he knew would happen between them—had to happen between them—more acceptable. The wild conflagration of desire was softening his brain, making him lose sight of the facts.

'I thought we might talk a walk in the hills, and you'll need walking shoes—something flat, anyway.' He fetched a knife and sliced the pizza. 'I guess we'll need the exercise after eating this!' he added drily, forcing himself to look anywhere but at her.

Fortunately, she'd packed a pair of flat canvas shoes, intending to explore the countryside to remove herself from his presence. It would be far nicer to explore it with him. Annie gave herself up to the glow of stolen happiness. Later, she'd try to puzzle out his increasingly incomprehensible behaviour.

He'd treated her like a tramp to begin with—a tramp he fancied, but otherwise regarded as being beneath contempt. Then that weird, lover-like act in front of Mark, and continuing to mildly flirt until he'd started the grand inquisition last night. And now he was acting like a particularly nice big brother—with the occasional tendency to snap.

She simply couldn't figure it out, so she wouldn't try just yet. For the next day or two she'd go with the flow—always remembering, of course, that he was promised to someone else, not letting herself fall into the trap and get any silly ideas...

Annie took the tiny sewing box from its hiding place in one of the drawers in the chest in her bedroom. She'd found it when she'd been putting her undies away. Surely no one would mind if she used it.

Taking it and the yellow shift dress she'd decided to wear when she had her business meeting with Signor Roselli over to the bed, she sank down on the pretty coverlet. On their return from their walk in the herb-scented hills, Daniel had suggested they both took a shower and rested up.

'It's been years, if not decades since I've been so idle,' he'd confessed, with the slightly self-deprecating smile that always turned her heart over. 'And I must admit I could get to like it!'

She'd almost sagged with relief. Parting company for what was left of the afternoon was a great idea. His was an overpowering presence, and her yearning for him was getting to be intolerable. Spending time with him was an unwise addiction.

So she'd showered, put on fresh undies—stretch blue lace briefs and a tiny, teasing bra to match—and she was now going to let down the hem of that dress.

She looked at the miniature pair of scissors in the box and wondered if they'd be sharp enough—and Daniel tapped lightly on the door and walked right in. For a second, Annie froze, just looked at him, at the flare of dull colour that momentarily stroked those hard, high cheekbones, at the haze of naked desire that she thought she could see beneath the suddenly hooded lids.

Then, as if someone had waved a magic wand, everything was back to normal—or as normal as it could be, considering, Annie thought wildly as he said tightly, 'I thought you'd like a long cold drink.'

She dragged the yellow dress up to cover her near nakedness and only then did she see that he was carrying a tall glass, full of pale liquid and clinking with ice cubes. That his dark hair was still damp from the shower, sticking to his head. That he was wearing brief white cotton shorts and nothing else.

Her throat was dry, her lips parched, her flesh trembling; she could feel it. He put the glass down on the bedside table. 'Lemonade.' His eyes clashed with hers, his voice harshly resonant as he deplored the lack of will that had allowed him to come to her room, his apparent powerlessness in the face of what now seemed inevitable. He cleared his throat, trying to get a grip on himself, and asked more gently, 'What are you doing?'

The ball was firmly in her court. Somehow she had to match his apparent insouciance, behave as if being naked together—or as near as dammit—in her bedroom was no big deal.

She lifted the glass, appalled by the way her hand was shaking, and sipped at the cold drink to clear the constriction in her throat. Then she managed, 'Trying to turn down the hem of a dress.' She gathered courage. He probably didn't know it, but he was making it easier for her. He wasn't looking at her now, but had padded across to the window, staring out, his shoulders high and rigid. She could think more clearly when she wasn't faced with the brooding intensity of his eyes. 'It's too short for a business meeting, I thought,' she told him, her voice commendably crisp. 'OK in every other way, though, I think—short sleeves, modest neckline. I don't want to make a bad impression on Signor Roselli.'

He swung round from the window, dark brows pulled down. He paced over to the bed. 'Stand up. Let me see.' This, at least, was something practical. He whipped the yellow shift from her shaky fingers, his features blank as he commanded again, 'Stand up, Annie.'

Dragging in a deep breath, praying her legs wouldn't give way under her, she did, swelteringly aware of all her exposed flesh, the brief undies that did nothing at all to hide anything! She couldn't breathe—air was locked tight inside her lungs and she couldn't let it out.

He held the dress against her. She clutched at it gratefully and wasn't as sure as she had been of his indifference. A tiny pulse was beating wildly at the side of his hard jaw and his voice was thicker than normal as he muttered, 'It looks fine to me. You have beautiful legs, Annie. Hiding them should be made a criminal offence.' He straightened up, still holding the soft yellow fabric against her shoulder. 'You talk about giving a bad impression, and earlier you thought your shoes were tarty. What's it all about?'

The need to know, to know everything about this witch of a woman, darkened his eyes, pulled his brows together. And she would tell him, ask his opinion, because it had begun to worry her—even though she had stubbornly vowed she could dress any way she liked.

Still holding the dress against her body, she felt for the edge of the bed and sat down. He joined her. She wished he hadn't, he was far too close for her peace of mind, but she couldn't tell him as much. It would only serve to remind him of what she'd said last night, the revealing confession of the effect his kisses and caresses had had on her.

'Well?' he prompted coolly.

'Rupert was always saying my clothes were blatant, and then Mark said he wanted me to go home with him as his guest because one look at me and Enid would give up the fight and go straight home. Though that's plain crazy, because she's beautiful. And you yourself,' she reminded him, 'said I was a menace to the whole male sex.'

Once in her stride she couldn't stop. She had never, in the whole of her life, opened up to anyone the way she had to him. As if she couldn't help herself, as if all the details of her life were being drawn from her with her willing co-operation.

And never in her adult life had she suffered from this unnerving lack of confidence in herself. 'After Aunt Tilly died and I was on my own I went ahead and did what I wanted to do; spending my money as fast as I earned it because I'd never had a sixpence to call my own before, dressing in the brightest colours I could find to wipe out the memory of brown and more brown—all those bunchy, shapeless things she made me wear,' she said glumly. 'Now I think I went over the top. It's come as a bit of a shock to find people think I'm easy because of the way I dress. Sorry,' she said, deeply ashamed now of her outburst. 'I'm not usually such a self-pitying wimp.'

'Annie—' Daniel reached out to touch the side of her face. He knew it was a mistake—she was coming over as Miss Sweetness and Light, and he was more than halfway to believing the myth, his emotions getting more involved than he wanted them to be—but, Lord help him, with Annie his body, his instincts, had a habit of taking over, blanking out his brain.

Her beautiful eyes locked with his—beautiful, deeply troubled eyes, wary, too, as his fingers stroked down to her delicate jawline. 'You are beautiful. All of you. Every last exquisite inch.' He rubbed his thumb softly over the luscious curve of her lower lip and felt her flesh tremble, and he couldn't stop himself because he knew now that he had to have her, all of her. He felt his own bones shake, desire surging, a hot, unstoppable tide of need.

He took the yellow fabric from her unresisting fingers, and devoured every tantalising curve, tasting every inch of her with his eyes. 'Don't ever change.' The command came from some unplumbed depth of his psyche. 'I want you just as you are.' He couldn't drag his eyes away from her wide and lustrous eyes, the parted, pouting lips, the enticing creamy swell of her breasts as they thrust against the lacy cloth. His heart thumped against his breastbone.

Dear God, but he had to have her! He shifted closer, his hands beginning to shake as they drifted to her fragile collarbones, afraid the strength of his passion would break her if he lost all control.

Annie's eyes closed in brief and cataclysmic ecstasy as her small hands covered his, pressing them closer to her heated flesh before, with a gesture of despair, she tugged them away.

'Don't! Get out of here! Leave me alone, Daniel. You may think it's OK to cheat on your future wife, but I don't.' She crossed her arms over her breasts, trying to hide from those dark, smoky eyes. When he looked at her like that it drove her wild, putting her in danger of forgetting the moral issue, taking the rapture he was offering because she couldn't live without it.

Smouldering eyes locked with hers. 'What did you say?' He looked utterly bemused, as if she'd spoken in a foreign language.

So he was lost in passion, too, Annie thought raggedly, wondering at the power of what they could do to each other. It was up to her to be the strong one. Difficult, but she had to try.

'I was reminding you—again,' she stressed, 'that there's a woman out there somewhere who doesn't deserve this. The woman you're going to marry. And I don't deserve it, either. I won't be your bit on the side, a little light entertainment while we're here together.'

She thought she'd handled it well, smothered the hurt, the need, the deep, deep ache. Glossed it over with a cool statement of fact. But he was grinning at her, his unforgettable features radiating determination and something else, right there in his eyes, which eluded her.

He was going to sweep aside all her objections, she knew he was, and she started to panic because she didn't know how long she could keep up the mental fight. He took her hands in his and pulled them up to his naked chest. The crisp hairs tickled the backs of her fingers and she swallowed raggedly, choking on a tight, hard sob.

'For a moment I didn't know what you were talking about,' he said quickly. Twice now she'd done this to them. Had his original assumption been right? Was she driving him to the brink and then holding him off, waiting to hear him tell her that his fiancée would soon be ex, that he wanted her instead? He wasn't about to give her the opportunity. Because he didn't want her to damn herself in his eyes all over again? Because he liked the way—against all the facts—he was beginning to believe in her?

He wasn't about to give that uncomfortable premise any headroom!

'There is no woman waiting in the background. For the past year there's been no woman at all. And during the four years before that just one brief and meaningless affair.'

And now he was about to embark on another. And he wouldn't have to fight for it; Annie was just as eager as he was. He remembered the sultry responsiveness of her body and his soul shuddered. He wanted her for himself. It had nothing to do with taking her away from his brother and keeping her away, and everything to do with craving the ecstasy, the earth-shattering release she alone could give him.

His fingers tightened around hers and he drew them up to his mouth, shifting his lean, hard body closer until she felt the heat of it scorch her flesh.

Sucking in her breath, she reminded him in a tinny, shaky voice, 'You said, at your cottage, that you'd have to look for something bigger when you married. I was there—I heard you. You can't deny it.'

'I'm not even going to try to!' He tried to curb his impatience. Did she want it in writing? 'Naturally I'd need a bigger place if I ever decided to marry and raise a family.' He unfurled her fingers and placed the tips against his mouth, his lips moving with slow-burning deliberation as he told her, 'There is no fiancée for me to cheat on, and that's the truth.' He was rapidly losing every scrap of control. He let it go— no regrets, just wild exhilaration.

He took both her hands in his, anchored them at the back of his neck and kissed her. Kissed her sultrily heavy eyelids, the curve of a cheekbone, the point of her jaw just beneath her ear and then her lips, slowly, softly parting them, sliding in the tip of his tongue, finding hers, and a shaft of exultancy pierced through him as the peaks of her breasts hardened against his pounding heart, burning his flesh.

The moan of surrender coming from the back of her throat was feral and intoxicating. Her need was as great as his. To hell with the rest. In this they were glorious equals. This gloriously sexy, fabulously lovely woman was his, and as she began to kiss him back, ferociously at first, as if she would devour him, body and soul, he had the wildly outrageous sensation that he had been born for this one moment alone.

His hands shook as he found the back fastening of her bra and allowed her beautiful, bountiful breasts their freedom. Swollen breasts, peaked with desire. He took one nipple into his mouth and suckled fiercely, his head snapping up at her high, wild cry.

'Annie—sweetheart—did I hurt you?' Remorse darkened his eyes. He would hate to think his driven, sexual hunger had caused her even the slightest pain. A deep need to pleasure her flooded right through him.

He moved his hands to cup her face, searching her eyes, and saw the wondering smile that curved her softly luscious lips as she moved his hands urgently down to her pouting breasts. 'Of course not.' Her smile was transformed into pure witchery. 'I just didn't know it could be so wonderful. Please. Again. More.'

I love you, she thought with a savage spurt of emotion as his mouth tugged at her engorged ripeness. More than you will ever know or I will ever be able to tell you. And her love went deeper, far deeper, than this physical expression—rapturous though it was. She knew now that she'd been tumbling fathoms deep ever since that kiss on a dark December night.

Her body shook feverishly when he eventually slid her briefs down the length of her legs, and her hands trembled as she helped him remove his shorts. Her body moved instinctively for him, opened for him, shaking now because she couldn't bear to disappoint him. Because from that single experience with Rupert she guessed she wasn't much good at this.

But her inhibitions only lasted a few moments before they dissolved as if she had never had them, and she wrapped her arms around his taut body, matching his movements as his flesh drove into the receptive sweetness of hers, in the rapturous, relentless journey to that place beyond the stars.

CHAPTER SEVEN

FOR Annie the next few days were an idyll, an enchanted time of long, hot days and warm, scented nights. And Daniel. Loving Daniel. And being brave enough, or stupid enough, to hope he felt the same.

Today they were to have their final meeting with Giovanni Roselli, she reminded herself. Not surprisingly, the small fact that this was supposed to be a business trip had flown out of her head, and she had never got round to letting down the hem of that yellow dress.

It didn't matter. Nothing mattered except her relationship with Daniel. Being with him, sharing, growing closer, surrounded by the ever-present, ever-fizzling sexual tension that broke in great floods of ecstatic release only to return with greater depth, greater intensity.

Annie got up from her hands and knees and tossed the wild mane of her hair back from her face before swirling her cloth in the bucket of hot soapy water and squeezing it out.

She'd already put the coffee on and started washing the kitchen floor before Daniel came down from the bedroom they now shared at seven o'clock.

'What do you think you're doing?' He sounded amused as he bent to pat her white shorts-clad rump, his voice deepening, thickening, as he clamped his hands on either side of her waist, hauled her to her feet and twisted her round to face him. 'I woke and reached for you but you weren't there. I'm feeling deprived,' he told her smokily, and began stroking the soft flesh above the waistband of her shorts.

Which made her feel deeply deprived, too. Which was his intention, judging by the look of devilish male purpose in his eyes. Any second now, his hands would move to the black cropped-off halter top she was wearing, removing it, releasing her tingling breasts to the honeyed, sweet pleasuring of his mouth. And if she raised her hands she could touch his naked chest, run her fingers over the crisp body hair, the rich tan of the slick skin that covered such impressive muscles, feel the drumbeat of his heart, slide down to the unbuttoned waistband of his jeans...

Later, she told herself. And she told him, 'Someone has to keep the place neat.'

'In Assunta's unavoidable absence I'm going to hire someone from the village—' his fingers tangled in her long hair, drawing it forward to cocoon them both, binding them together in a cascade of crinkly sunshine '—to clean the place through when we leave. How about that?'

That sultry, come-to-bed tone sent shudders of need snaking through her. He surely was the male embodiment of temptation. 'Fine,' she said sternly. 'In the meantime, humour me. I woke up this morning and turned over a new leaf. I no longer have the need to live in a pig sty. I'm practising for when I get back to my place and put my long-suffering flatmate out of her misery.'

She placed her hands on his shoulders and stood
on her toes to put a placatory kiss on his lips. And
that was a hopelessly wrong move, because, moving
closer, raising her body, he fitted the evidence of his
desire snugly between her thighs.

His groan of pleasure almost made her good intentions fly out of her head. But she felt the tell-tale
trembling of her flesh, the pooling of heat deep inside
her, and twisted away just in time, releasing them both
from the bright cocooning cloak of her hair.

Back down on her hands and knees, reaching for
the floor cloth, babbling because he wouldn't—he
surely wouldn't—would he? 'I have to tell you that
when I was on my own, after my aunt died, I rebelled.
Not only over what I wore, and leaving my hair out
of its braid, but in my surroundings.' She rubbed ferociously at the floor tiles. 'Her house was Spartan.
Spotless. There was a place for everything. I wasn't
allowed to leave so much as a book lying around. So,
as well as letting my hair blow free, and buying outrageous clothes, I never had a place for anything—
and if by mishap I did, then the right thing wasn't in
it!' She sat back on her haunches and swished the
cloth around in the soapy water. 'I've grown out of
the need to rebel,' she told him, her pansy eyes suddenly serious. Then, 'There's fresh coffee in the pot,'
she said, dismissing the subject. 'Help yourself. I'll
join you soon. I won't be long.'

'Don't be,' he ordered, pouring coffee now, his
tone indulgent, amused. 'And don't turn yourself into
Mrs Mop. Or I might not love you any more!'

Grinning, he strode out to the terrace and stopped

short. His eyes fixed on the impressive view, not seeing it, any of it, and the smile was wiped from his face, fading from his eyes.

Did he love her? It had been meant as a teasing joke. But was it the truth? He didn't know. It was a shock to a guy's system. Carefully, he put his untouched coffee down on the table and went like a sleepwalker to the edge of the terrace, still staring at the view, still not seeing it.

Annie set to work again, her thoughts wistful. He hadn't meant that he loved her. He'd been teasing her about her new-found interest in house cleaning. Anything else—like his lifelong love and devotion— was too much for her to hope for.

But she wasn't going to brood about it. Of course she wasn't. Why spoil something that was so wonderful? She loved him; that had to be enough. She would take what she could of him, gratefully accept the joy and the rapture, and do her crying—if she had to—later.

After she'd stowed the bucket and cloth away, she washed her hands, eyed the coffee pot and decided she didn't want any. She wanted Daniel.

Allowing herself to admit she loved him had given her an undreamt of freedom. The freedom not to rebel against the earlier, unhappier part of her life. The freedom to be herself and not the antithesis of everything her aunt had expected her to be. But, most of all, the freedom to express her love for Daniel—if not in words, then in deeds.

Most definitely in deeds, she thought, her heart storming around beneath her breasts, her pulses skittering in helpless anticipation as she walked softly across the terrace, discarding her top as she went, dropping it carelessly on the ground as she crossed to where he was standing, apparently engrossed in the view. She pressed her naked breasts against the broad expanse of his tanned back, wrapping her arms around him and sliding her fingers beneath the casually unfastened waistband of his jeans.

For a moment his body went taut, very still, muscles contracting. And then he turned with a growl of triumph and scooped her up in his arms and carried her back to bed, those troubled thoughts and unanswerable questions deserting him completely.

'You look great—Tuscany obviously agreed with you!' Sally wandered into the main office, a file in her hands. 'Congratulations on pulling off your first deal!'

'Thanks.' Annie returned the warm smile, blushing. Not at the praise, but because her thoughts were churning around in an alarming mixture of nerves and helplessly hopeful anticipation.

Barnes had met them at the airport last evening and Daniel had kissed her lingeringly while the chauffeur was getting her luggage from the boot and carrying it up to the doorstep. 'Dinner tomorrow night,' he'd promised huskily. 'I'll pick you up at eight. We need to talk, get a few things sorted out.'

She'd lain awake most of the night, missing him terribly, forcing herself to accept that over dinner tonight he might be aiming to break it to her that their brief affair had been no more than a holiday fling. If he did then she was going to have to accept it, take it on the chin, and not embarrass him by going to pieces. She would do that in privacy.

But she couldn't help hoping…

'If you looked the way you do today, it's no wonder you got such a good deal!' Sally said, envy and admiration scrambled up in her tone.

Annie took the file and tried to hide her inner agitation. Truth to tell, her meetings with Signor Roselli were something of a blur, fading into insignificance beside the wonderful magic of being in love, really and deeply in love for the very first time. Just Daniel was burned indelibly into her memory of that week in Tuscany; the way he looked, his voice, the things he said, the way he reached out to touch her at every opportunity, making meals together, laughter and wine and long, soft, dark nights of love.

On the flight home yesterday Daniel had assured her she'd made a fantastic deal. But then, Daniel had still been on a high from nearly a week of mindblowing, fabulous sex. Mark might think differently.

As soon as Sally left the office Annie checked that her stocking seams were straight. She wanted to look perfectly groomed and controlled when her boss arrived. She loved the drama of her narrow white skirt topped by a sleeveless black silk blouse, plain black court shoes and a scarlet belt around her tiny waist. But maybe she should seriously consider toning down the way she dressed. Yet hadn't Daniel said he liked her just the way she was?

She hadn't time to think about that right now. She

was going to have to make her peace with Mark. Somehow.

He'd advised her to consolidate her relationship with his brother and she'd thought terrible things of him, said terrible things to him, and as good as handed in her resignation. He wasn't to know she'd got it into her head that Daniel was soon to be married!

She hoped her boss would overlook her rabid outburst. No wonder he'd looked as if a bomb had dropped on his head!

'Got over your temper?' Mark asked when he walked into his office half an hour later.

'I'm sorry, truly I am,' Annie said quickly. 'You see—I—'

'Forget it.' He cut her short. 'I'm sure your explanation's too confused for a mere male to follow. So I'll do us both a favour and put it down to hormones. Can I take it you've decided to stay?' Without waiting for an affirmative, taking it for granted, he got down to business. 'So tell me how it went. Dan faxed through details of the deal on Monday. It looks pretty good to me. Shall we go through it?'

Annie did her best to switch her brain into business mode, but it was difficult. Her mind kept turning to the coming evening. Daniel had said they needed to talk, they had things to sort out. She felt alternately excited and hopeful, momentarily believing that he'd tell her he wanted their relationship to continue, and then sick and cold inside because she was sure he wouldn't.

When Sally carried their coffee through at eleven Mark leaned back in his chair. 'Let's take a break.'

He tipped his head on one side and gave her an encouraging smile. 'Now tell me, how did you and my big brother get along? Sorted yourselves out, I hope?'

Annie concentrated on serving them both from the coffee pot, passing him the cream and sugar. She didn't need an inquisition. She didn't want to share the precious secret of her love for Daniel with anyone, not even his brother.

Yet how to fob him off without sounding churlish? It made her feel guilty, especially as he'd so generously forgiven her ferocious outburst. She should have foreseen this happening—provided, of course, Mark hadn't thrown her off the premises for her gross insubordination of a week ago—should have thought out what to say should he start to probe.

'I guess.' Discomfort made her voice colder than she'd intended, and, from Mark's heavy sigh, had given entirely the opposite impression to what had actually happened. She shifted uneasily in her chair.

'Which means you didn't,' Mark said heavily. 'Listen, I can understand if you're still angry with him for what he did on the night of my mother's party, the way he—' His face went pink as he stirred his coffee far too vigorously. 'The way he took advantage of you. Would it help if I told you why he did it?'

Annie hid a smile. She had never seen Mark embarrassed before. She nodded her bright head. She and Daniel had never really discussed her kidnapping—they'd had far too many much more enjoyable things on their minds—but, from what she could piece together, he'd taken her off the scene to leave Enid a clear field. He'd seen her as a threat, as Mark had intended his entire family, plus Enid, to do, and removed her! But it would be amusing to find out how Mark viewed his brother's actions.

'He was protecting me,' Mark said. 'Unlike Ma, who did it ad nauseam for years, he would never stuff Enid's suitability as a wife down my throat. So I knew it wasn't that. At first I took it at face value, that the two of you had taken one look at each other and dived headlong into a mad, passionate affair. But your attitude, the things you said, told me you couldn't face up to what had happened, couldn't forgive him for what he'd done.

'When he dropped by that morning to return your nightdress and make plans for that trip you froze him off, and when you knew he would be with you in Tuscany you went hysterical—which is totally unlike you—and threatened to resign.'

He pushed his empty coffee cup over the table and Annie dutifully refilled it, taking her time, her mind flying back to that night at the cottage, because Mark's use of those words 'protecting me' jangled a few alarm bells.

That tied in with the things Daniel had said. That he didn't want to see his brother involved with someone like her was just one of them. Unconsciously, she shook her head. She was being silly. 'Well, tell me more,' she said lightly. 'Why think he was protecting you? It seems a peculiar choice of word.'

Mark shook his head. 'Not really, not when you know the background. Believe me, it's totally unlike Dan to do anything off the top of his head. He thinks long and hard before he acts, uses that cool, precise brain of his—he's famous for it!'

Annie couldn't rise to his attempt to lighten an atmosphere that suddenly seemed to be swirling with dark undercurrents. What was this 'background' he'd mentioned—as if it was something too dreadful to talk about? Why didn't he get to the point?

She didn't have to wait long before Mark blew the lid off her happy fantasy. He gave her a long, level look and said, 'Five years ago I met Lorna Fox and was completely and utterly bowled over. She was like you. Not in looks—she had long, silky straight red hair and the greenest eyes I've ever seen—but very similar in the way she held herself, her provocative walk, the aura around her. She was full of life, fizzling, colourful. Like you, she'd never get lost in a crowd. She was loving, and generous with her loving. Too generous,' he said, with a touch of old bitterness. 'We got engaged and I was the happiest man on God's earth. This was before Dan helped me get started up on my own, and I was out of the country for long stretches of time.

'When I got back from a two-month trip to the Far East I found a couple of surprises waiting for me. The first was a message on my answer-machine from Lorna, saying she was in Scotland on holiday with friends, that she'd get in touch when she got back to London, but she wasn't sure when that would be. The second was a phone call from Dan, inviting me to have dinner with him and his brand-new fiancée the next evening.'

Annie was far from stupid—discounting the Tuscan

idyll. She knew what was coming. Why else would Mark have stressed her likeness to that other woman, Lorna? Her body tensed. She felt nauseous. She didn't want to hear any more, wanted her fantasy intact, wanted the delicious excitement of occasionally allowing herself to believe that things would work out for her and Daniel. But it was all already unwinding around the edges, and she had to steel herself to take what was coming next.

'And, yes, you've probably guessed it—Lorna Fox was Dan's brand-new fiancée. In retrospect, the look on her face when I walked into that restaurant was hilarious. She hadn't made the connection—Dan and I have different fathers, different surnames, remember. It turned out that shortly after I'd left on that protracted business trip she and Dan attended the same cocktail party. She made sure they were introduced and bingo! She could bewitch any man she decided she wanted. Conveniently, she hadn't been wearing my ring—it would have been a big hindrance to a woman on the prowl.

'At first she put on the act of her life—all tearful innocence. She and Daniel had met and she'd realised her mistake in promising to marry me. She would have told me and returned my ring. She was going to find it hard to hurt me—hence the lie about being in Scotland—she needed time to work up enough courage.

'When it sank in that both Dan and I wanted nothing more to do with her, she lost it. Then the truth really came out. I was, so she told me, quite a catch. A highly paid job, my own apartment in London, a well-heeled family in the background. But Dan was a much better one, financially. Why shouldn't a girl take the best offer she could get? Perhaps now you can understand why he did what he did?

Mark was waiting for an affirmative. She couldn't give it. Not that she didn't understand his motives now; she did. Only too well. She stared at the coffee cup she still held in her hands, frozen, unable to say a word, misery tearing her to pieces.

As if he believed she hadn't got the picture, needed to drive his defence of his brother's indefensible actions further home, he said, 'Look at it from his point of view. You'd been engaged to one of his key employees, and he wasn't to know that when you kissed him at that party it was a case of mistaken identity. Then you turned up with me and he thought what I'd *intended* they should all think—and for that, Annie, I'll never be able to apologise enough.

'Dan obviously thought history was repeating itself and took action to split us up. The Lorna affair affected me badly. Dan handled it much better, but I felt as if my whole world had fallen apart. I'm sure he now knows he misjudged you badly. Well, of course he does—why else would he have wanted you with him in Tuscany? Can't you understand, and forgive him?'

She could understand, but she couldn't forgive. Neither could she forgive herself for jumping headlong into a fool's paradise, allowing the potent addiction of his lovemaking to blur her mind, making her forget or at the very best totally discount all that had happened before, the questions that had remained unanswered because she'd been too besotted to ask them.

And Mark had got it wrong. She knew the real reason for the Tuscan adventure. He'd needed to brand her. Almost as if he'd known, from her earlier wild responses, that she'd be spoiled for any other man after him. He'd wanted to make sure he could keep his brother out of her clutches. Why else would he have appeared that morning, waving her discarded nightie like a chequered flag, acting like a lover, flirting with her until, safely at the old farmhouse, he'd stared to be so darned nice, lulling her into a false sense of security before he went in for the kill?

Suddenly aware that Mark was still waiting for some response, she forced herself to smile, albeit weakly, got to her feet and began putting the cups back on the tray.

'Thanks for putting me in the picture.' It felt like thanking someone for pushing a knife in her heart. 'I can't imagine why he didn't simply take you on one side and warn you. Come straight out with it and tell you he thought I was another Lorna,' she said stiffly, wondering how she could get through the rest of the day.

'Oh, I can!' Mark grinned at her. 'I worked that out a while back.' He pulled a file towards him and opened it, his head bent over it as he asked idly, 'So when are you seeing him again?'

'Tonight.'

'Good.'

There was nothing remotely good about it.

They wouldn't be sharing the intimate dinner for

two she'd been so looking forward to and 'sorting things out'. So she could stop wildly fantasising—in her sillier moments—about the possibility of him confessing his love for her, proposing marriage and the two of them discussing the wedding. Where and when, the wonderful future they were to share together, creating the close, loving family she'd always dreamed about. She was just as foolish as Aunt Tilly had always said.

He had probably decided he'd done his duty and got her out of Mark's hair. He'd give her a civilised dinner, say, Nice while it lasted, have a good life, and that would be that.

Only it wouldn't be like that, she assured herself as she crossed to her desk in the corner of the room and opened a new file on the computer. She would get in first. Hurt him for hurting her.

Normally she wasn't a vengeful creature, but there was always a first time. Love and hate and bitter hurt changed everything. She didn't know how she'd do it, but she'd come up with something.

Thankfully, Cathy had a date, and rushed back from work, showered and changed and rushed out again. Annie wouldn't have to tell Daniel Faber to get lost in front of an audience.

She changed into a pair of washed-out old jeans and an ancient T-shirt that should have been thrown in the dustbin ages ago, scrubbed every scrap of make-up off her face and laboriously braided her hair.

Seeing her in her grunge, not looking at all special

for him, would be the opening salvo in her war of attrition.

She didn't want to fight with him. She wanted to love him for the rest of her life. But that wasn't an option because he certainly didn't love her. At least he hadn't lied about that.

Tears filled her eyes, but she brushed them angrily away, swallowing the lump in her throat, making herself remember the things she'd conveniently shut out of her head when she'd found herself falling in love with him.

If she'd had her wits about her she would have known what he was up to. His voice echoed in her mind, the things he'd said coming back to haunt her.

'I can't stop you being a menace to the male sex. But don't mess with my family...'

'I don't want to see Mark get romantically involved with someone like you.'

'You're on the loose again, but don't try to get your claws into me.'

'You wouldn't be averse to ditching Mark and moving up the ladder of financial security—I saw what you did to Rupert Glover.'

He'd said it all, and she'd been too stupid to see the motivation behind his words. And later too besotted. Besotted, stupid females lost all judgement, and the ease with which he'd disarmed her into getting into his car on the night of the party should have told her what he was capable of.

She watched the hands of the clock mark off the passing minutes with hollow misery. She felt sick and shivery and wanted nothing more than to give in to cowardice, climb into bed and pull the covers over her head.

Would Daniel break the door down if she refused to answer? Or camp on the doorstep until Cathy came back and let him in?

No, of course not; he would do nothing of the sort. He wasn't the ardent lover of her soppy imaginings. Sure, he'd made love to her, and why not? She'd been rather more than willing and he hadn't been averse to killing two birds with one stone. Getting her away from Mark *and* slaking the lust that had always been there.

So if she didn't answer the door he'd go away. Annoyed at having wasted his time, washing his hands of the concept of telling her goodbye over a civilised meal.

'You were right about me, Aunt Tilly,' she said into the silence, the sound of her own voice helping to strengthen her resolve to tell him to get out of her life before he told her to get out of his. 'Acknowledge your failings, my girl,' she muttered to herself, 'and you're halfway to beating them.'

Or was she? When the doorbell rang she wasn't so sure. She felt as stupid as ever, her bones dissolving, her heart jumping up into her throat and choking her. The desire to leave him on the doorstep warred with her need to see him this one last time, assert herself, prove she wasn't foolish, not any more.

Forcing her legs to move, she made it out to the lobby, frantically told herself she could handle this, and opened the door.

He looked devastating, the white dinner jacket enhancing the tan he'd so easily acquired in Italy, the long, tightly muscled legs encased in narrow black trousers, that slightly lop-sided half-smile something she now dreaded because it was so incredibly sexy... She almost flew into his arms, praying for a miracle. But she stopped herself because miracles didn't happen, planted her feet apart and stuck her hands on her hips.

'You'd prefer to spend the evening in?' Daniel asked softly, aching to take her in his arms. She looked so adorable, mussed and slightly pink, the ancient jeans and T-shirt doing nothing to lessen the impact of her sizzling sex appeal.

He'd asked Barnes to wait. Their table was booked at one of the most fashionable restaurants in the city, the Dom Pérignon was already on ice, and the solitaire diamond ring he'd picked out from the selection brought over to his office by two uniformed security men this morning was safely in his pocket.

But if she wanted to cook for him, to spend a quiet evening at home, just the two of them, then that was better than fine by him! He'd actually prefer it. He could propose to her, tell her how completely and utterly he loved and adored her, just as well in private— better—as in a public place.

God, how he loved this woman! Loved the outgoing generosity of her spirit, her zest for life. The knowledge had hit him on the flight home. Suddenly he had known that she was none of the things he had so insultingly accused her of being. No promiscuous trollop could have been so untutored in the art of making love as she had been that first time—and he should have admitted his mistakes there and then, acknowledged that he must have been falling in love with her ever since he'd first seen her at Edward Ker's retirement party.

His smile faded, a slight frown pulling his brows together now. The colour had leached out of her skin, and for the first time he noticed the dark shadows beneath her eyes. Had Mark worked her ragged on her first day back in the office after her week away, making her catch up on all the accumulated paperwork?

A huge wave of protectiveness swallowed him up, churning his guts and making his heart ache ferociously. His brother could darn well look for another PA, starting tomorrow! She would be back to being her old bright-eyed and bushy-tailed self in time for the wedding—which would take place just as soon as everything could be arranged.

A huge wedding, with all the trimmings and then some. He wanted the whole world to marvel at his beautiful bride, his precious Annie!

He moved forward, but she, seemingly rooted to the spot, blocked his way. 'Annie?' His voice was throaty. What had happened to the radiant love of his life in the last twenty-four hours?

Her eyes flicked from his, down to his mouth. Her own lips trembled. He watched her compress them, stare at a point just beyond his left shoulder.

Her confrontational stance had changed to one of self-containment, her arms wrapped protectively around her gorgeous body. Something had happened. Something was wrong. Whatever it was, he would sort it. Nothing would be allowed to hurt or worry her, not while he was around to take care of her!

'Annie—' He reached out a hand to touch the side of her face, withdrawing it immediately when she flinched. His frown deepened. 'Something's wrong. Give me a second to send Barnes on his way, then we'll go inside and get it sorted out.'

'No!' she countermanded thinly, fighting her own demons. Perhaps he wanted to prolong their affair for a few short weeks, just to make sure she'd leave his brother alone! Well, she wasn't playing! She had worked out exactly what to say to make him leave her alone.

'You'll need your driver,' she informed him tonelessly. 'I don't want to see you any more and I can tell you why in just a few seconds.' She dragged in a painful breath. This was going to hurt her far more than it would hurt him. But it was the only way. He was an addiction, and her pride wouldn't let her become permanently hooked, a pathetic, clinging creature living in dread of the day when he would walk away.

'You were quite right about me. But then you're used to being right, aren't you? So it won't come as a shock.' She didn't look at him. She couldn't. She couldn't trust herself not to hurl herself into his arms and take what she could—an hour, a week, whatever.

'Truth is, I'm obviously a clone of Lorna Fox. There's someone else.' He couldn't think worse of her than he already did, so she was going for broke. In his mind she was already like Lorna Fox, always had been—a woman on the make, uncaring of who she trod on with her pretty stiletto heels on her upward journey.

'He's not as good to look at as you, and nowhere near as sexy. But he's much older and absolutely loaded. Last week was fun, but this other guy happens to be a good few rungs above you on the ladder and I don't think he'll want to be kept dangling very much longer. So, sorry, but a girl's got to do what a girl's got to do!' She bared her teeth in an empty smile, piling lie on top of terrible lie, sticking the knife in before he could stick it in her. 'Plus, he's got a title.'

He couldn't have registered that last outrageous untruth. He had gone very still, his face grey with shock. Then his eyes had gone hard, and now he was striding across the pavement. She didn't wait to watch him get into the chauffeur-driven Daimler, but pushed the door shut behind her and managed to reach the bathroom before she parted company with her lunch.

CHAPTER EIGHT

IT WAS the first really autumnal day of the season. Annie had woken to the sound of muted birdsong and the view from her window of a mist hanging over the garden, blurring outlines and softening hard edges, lying in swathes over the well-tended rosebeds and borders, twining through the branches of the trees.

She still couldn't believe she was actually here, here with Mark at his parents' home. She had never imagined herself to have so much courage.

His invitation had come like a bombshell, shattering the quiet order of his office on Thursday morning, making her stare at him with her mouth hanging open.

'Visit my folks with me this weekend, Annie? We can finish up here early tomorrow afternoon and drive down, have two full days there. It's lovely at this time of year. And it would do you good. You've been looking off colour ever since you got back from Tuscany.'

It had taken a full sixty seconds for Annie to get over the shock and sense of outrage and find her voice. It had come out strained, almost squeaky. 'After what happened last time? In your dreams! What on earth would your parents think if I had the gall to show my face there again? They won't want a repeat visit from the house guest from hell!' How could he be insensitive enough to suggest such a thing?

She pulled the cover off her computer and switched

it on. Sometimes, as now, she wondered if she should look for another job. Seeing Mark on a day-to-day basis reminded her too sharply of his brother, making him even more impossible to forget than he already was.

Mark crossed the room to stand behind her. He put his hands on her shoulders and pulled her round to face him. Over the past three weeks she'd been looking unbelievably tired and strained.

'The invitation initially came from my parents,' he assured her quietly. 'I told them everything—confessed to the lot, explained the whys and wherefores of everything that had happened. They were appalled to think they'd bred two such duplicitous sons! They want to give you a nice relaxed weekend to make up for what their devious, scheming sons put you through! They didn't have time to get to know you when you visited before, and they both insist that they want to.'

Annie set her soft mouth in a stubborn line. She was relieved to hear that the Redways didn't think badly of her after all. The way she'd apparently sneaked away in the night had bothered her. She had wanted to apologise and try to explain, but hadn't known how. Now Mark had done it for her and they'd understood. They were obviously more intelligent and open-minded than their elder son!

'That's nice of them. Please tell them I appreciate the invitation,' she dismissed, shrugging her shoulders free. 'Another time, maybe.'

'Not good enough, Annie.' He followed her over to one of the filing cabinets. 'Don't you think it's time you laid a few ghosts to rest? Besides, Enid's also anxious to get to know you better.' He looked slightly shamefaced, and shuffled his feet. 'You might as well be one of the first to know. We're getting engaged next month, on her birthday. It's odd, but I don't think I ever really saw her until that weekend. Now I can't really believe I could have been so blind for so many years.'

'That's wonderful news, Mark! I'm really happy for you both,' Annie said sincerely. She had taken to Enid immediately, and in any other circumstances would have liked to have her as a friend.

'So why don't you come down with me and tell her yourself?' Mark insisted. 'She gave me a message to pass on to you—she said, "Tell Annie, thank you; it worked." I suppose you know what she means. She refused to explain to me!'

'Then I don't think I will, either.' Annie actually managed the first genuine smile in weeks. She was really pleased that Enid and Mark had found each other at last, and that her advice had helped bring it about. It would be nice to see the other girl, wish her long life and happiness. Nice to be part of a warm, friendly family if only for a couple of days. She was still working on resigning herself to the fact that she would never have one of her own, learning to live with the certain knowledge that she'd never fall in love again.

She was tempted, though, to take up the invitation, but... 'Will Daniel be there?' she asked stiffly, ready to decline immediately, no hope of anyone changing her mind, if he was.

Mark turned back to his desk, opening his briefcase and shuffling through the contents. 'Dan's in Brussels; he certainly won't be weekending with the folks. I've hardly seen him since he got back from Italy.'

It was the first time Daniel's name had been mentioned by either of them since Mark had revealed the true motivations behind his brother's devious and cruel actions. Mark probably thought there was no further point in pursuing the matter of her forgiveness. He didn't know the full story, and unless Daniel told him, which he probably wouldn't, he never would.

Which suited her fine, and what he had said did gel. The two men didn't live in each other's pockets, rarely saw each other except for family occasions, and Daniel didn't interfere with his brother's business, didn't pop in and out of the office to check up on his investment.

Except for that one time. And she knew all too well what had brought that about, knew it wouldn't be repeated.

'OK, I'll come,' she said.

The visit would be a conclusion, and when it was over she could draw a final line under the most traumatic period of her life.

So now here she was, and so far her visit couldn't have been more pleasant. Annie turned from the window and went to the bathroom to shower. She was in the room she'd been given that first time, and surprisingly felt comfortably at home in it. Probably because she knew Daniel wouldn't appear, knew that this time there were no hidden agendas.

She stepped under the warm, refreshing spray, glad

now that she had found the courage to face them all again. When she and Mark had arrived at the end of Friday afternoon, he and his father had set up the barbecue on the terrace while she and his mother sat and watched them, sipping cool white wine.

'I can't tell you how glad I am you came,' Molly Redway had said. 'After what those hulking brutes of mine did I wouldn't blame you if you'd washed your hands of the lot of us. Men! They think they know everything, can make things happen simply because they decide they want them to be that way—as if no one else has an opinion worth listening to. Playing God, I call it! When most of them haven't got the sense they were born with!'

'Talking about me, by any chance?' Mark had wandered over to refill his and his father's glasses with wine, taking in most of his mother's scornful tirade. He'd quirked one eyebrow humorously at his unrepentant parent.

'If the cap fits!' She poked his taut tummy with a forefinger. 'Fancy making Annie come here under false pretences— the poor girl must have felt perfectly dreadful. I'm only too happy to know your scheming rebounded on you!'

'So am I, Ma,' he grinned. 'So am I! I stand repentant and suitably chastened.' He waved the wine bottle in front of them. 'A top-up, girls?'

'Don't change the subject. We're perfectly capable of helping ourselves. What I want to know is what the brute did to you, Annie, to make you agree to the silly idea in the first place.'

Annie glanced up at Mark. A tricky question. She

could hardly admit to having had a fellow sufferer's sympathy with someone who was constantly being pushed down a path he didn't want to travel. It would make Molly feel guilty, to blame for it all, and she didn't want that.

'He twisted my arm.' She smiled seraphically up at him, laying the blame where she felt it rightly belonged. 'He is my boss, after all. I do what he says, or he doesn't pay my wages!'

To give him his due, Mark accepted the calumny with good grace, departing swiftly to help his father at the barbecue, and Molly, her pretty, plump face wreathed in contented smiles, said, 'Enid told me you'd advised her to ignore Mark completely at my birthday party, fasten on another man and flirt with him like crazy.

'She knew then, of course, that you couldn't be romantically interested in Mark, but she was sure Mark was interested in you—how could he not have been, when you're so lovely? She almost decided against taking your advice, she told me. Only at the last minute she decided to give it a try. Nothing else had worked and she had nothing to lose—Mark never seemed aware of her existence unless she pushed herself under his nose, and then he treated her like a nice but slightly irritating little sister!

'And it did work—and I'm so happy about it I could burst! I always knew she was the right woman for him, but, typically, Mark wouldn't listen. They're so different, those sons of mine,' she confided, shaking her head. 'Mark leaps before he thinks—hence the hare-brained scheme to bring you down here, pretending you were the new woman in his life—while I'm sometimes afraid that Daniel does nothing *but* think!'

It had been the only time his name had been mentioned. Whether the Redways were being tactful or had wiped the whole episode from their minds, Annie didn't know, and she certainly wasn't going to ask.

The next day, Saturday, had been wet. Mark had left early to fetch Enid over to stay until Sunday evening. When she'd arrived she had given Annie a huge hug. She was looking so happy and relaxed that Annie's eyes had gone misty. At least one story had a happy ending.

But she hadn't come here to brood. There was plenty to do, even if the weather kept them indoors. Mark's father had gone to potter in his greenhouse, Mark had disappeared into the study to use the phone, and Enid and Annie had helped Molly prepare lunch, then sat in the kitchen over coffee discussing wedding arrangements.

Annie had forced herself not to mind, to enter into the spirit of it all. Her own stupid fantasies about marriage had come to nothing, but she couldn't let that stop her from enjoying the prospect of Enid and Mark's happiness at the coming event.

The happy couple were to be married in December, and the three of them had debated the choice of sleek white satin or fine white velvet—the latter being warmer and more fitted to the season, and the perniciously cold village church, but the former probably suiting Enid's delicate, slender figure rather better.

'I could always wear long johns!' Enid had giggled. 'And leg-warmers!'

Mark had walked in, looking edgy, helping himself wordlessly to coffee which he then took to the window, staring out at the rain.

'Wretched damn weather!' he'd practically snarled. 'Has anyone heard a forecast?'

Enid had shot him an anxious look, then hurriedly smiled at Annie. Molly had said, 'No, I haven't. Does it matter? We're enjoying ourselves, in spite of it. Take a coffee out to Father, would you, darling? He always forgets to come in for it. And tell him lunch at one sharp.'

At least today, Sunday, was dry, Annie thought now as she padded across from the bathroom, wrapped in a towel, to sit herself in front of the dressing table. She plugged in the hairdryer, thoughtfully provided, and got to work on the long, heavy mass.

Mark had seemed preoccupied with the state of the weather yesterday, getting increasingly edgy when the persistent rain had shown no signs of easing off. And twice she'd come across him and Enid, deep in low, earnest conversation, quickly broken off on her appearance.

Annie stopped thinking about it. If Mark had an almost pathological dislike of being housebound on a wet day that was Enid's problem, not hers.

As soon as her hair was almost dry Annie shed the towel. She braided her hair firmly, put on white cotton undies, a pair of peg-top grey cotton trousers and a slightly darker plain cotton shirt, and went down to breakfast.

'You look like a prison warder! But a gorgeously pretty one,' Mark added in the same breath, grinning, softening the criticism.

'Thank you—I think!' Annie gave him a cool look. This was her new persona, and everyone had better get used to it. She still couldn't bring herself to cut her hair, but she was replacing her wardrobe as and when she could afford to. Her outrageous style of dressing had landed her in a load of trouble and she was not going to let it happen again.

She helped herself to toast and honey and Molly, pouring from the chased silver coffee pot, asked, 'What are you planning to do today, Father?'

'Dead-heading the roses, for a start. So if anyone feels like helping—'

'Enid and I thought we'd take Annie to see Bull Farm,' Mark cut in. 'We could take the scenic route, park the car and approach it through the woods, now the weather's brightened up. If we take a picnic lunch we could eat it there.' He turned to Annie, explaining, 'The farm's being sold piecemeal at auction. The house itself would make a perfect family home. It's structurally sound, has fantastic views, and that particular lot includes a three-acre garden and another three of woodland,' he finished off enthusiastically.

So that explained yesterday's annoyance over the rain, the excitement in his eyes, the smile that Enid suddenly couldn't seem to stop. They wanted her to see what they hoped would be their future home, to walk through the woods that might become their own and see it all in comfort without getting soaked.

'But I thought you and Enid said you'd prefer to

live in town!' Molly said, throwing up her hands in a gesture that said she couldn't keep up with the vagaries of the younger generation. 'And I'm sure I heard that someone has stepped in and bought the actual farmhouse, and it's just the pastureland that's to go to public auction.'

'Shall Annie and I make up a packed lunch?' Enid put in quickly, getting to her feet to clear the table now that everyone had finished.

Mark got up to help her and his mother said, 'I suppose you know your own minds—even if you do change them as often as you change your underwear! And if you're tramping through the woods, Annie will need to borrow a pair of my wellington boots. I'll help you in the garden, Father. I love dead-heading roses. I can look at the blooms that are left and think nice peaceful thoughts!'

The borrowed boots were on the big side. Annie's feet were slithering around inside them. But she could see the necessity. Yesterday's rain had made the ground decidedly sticky.

The sun had finally broken through the early mist, adding to the increasingly festive atmosphere that was infecting her two companions. Mark had parked the car in a convenient pull-in at the side of the narrow lane and Enid had hustled her through a boarded door set in a high stone wall.

'Is this the woodland that goes with the house you've got your eye on?' Annie asked, picking her way carefully along the trodden muddy track.

'Great, isn't it?' Mark enthused. 'Covered in bluebells and wild garlic in spring, a lovely peaceful place—and safe for children to play in.'

It was almost as if he were trying to sell her the property, instead of wanting to buy it for himself and his soon-to-be bride, Annie thought, smiling to herself at this enthusiasm for all things rural. She had always thought him such an urban man, needing bright city lights, theatres and restaurants, a busy social life.

'Clean air for them to breathe, too,' Enid burbled behind her on the narrow track, and Annie wondered if the other girl was pregnant already. Was that the reason for this sudden fixation on ideal surroundings for a young family?

She could hardly ask. It would seem like prying, and if that *were* the case she wouldn't be able to help a stab of envy. They loved each other, had their sights firmly set on the ideal family home, and all this emphasis on how perfect it would be for children must mean that they were already planning a large family. The excitement that fizzed between the two only went to confirm it.

But she wouldn't be mean-minded and envious, she told herself firmly. She would be happy for them, and not let her own shattered dreams and broken heart turn her into a sour, jealous kill-joy.

So when Mark, walking ahead of her, stopped and muttered, 'Oh, hell, we left the picnic in the car! I'll have to go back and fetch it,' she could only smile wistfully, because their excitement at taking her to see the home they wanted to acquire had made them forget the hamper of food and the basket containing the bottle of wine, glasses and corkscrew Enid had insisted they needed to make the outing complete.

For herself she had no such excuse for forgetting the picnic things, except that on the drive to where they'd left the car she'd been painfully reminded of the countryside she'd glimpsed when Barnes had driven her away from Daniel's weekend cottage. She hadn't been able to get him out of her head.

But she was working on it, and it helped when Enid offered, 'I'll come with you, darling, and help carry it all.'

'We can't leave Annie on her own,' Mark objected, perhaps too quickly. 'And I'm sure she won't want to trail all the way down to the car and back again.'

Catching the hopeful look in his eyes, Annie said, 'Of course you can leave me on my own. Go ahead, both of you. I'm not likely to be eaten by bears, am I?' He probably wanted this unlooked for opportunity to have his Enid to himself for ten minutes—a supposition borne out when he stepped around her and took Enid's hand in his.

'Well, if you're sure? Carry on up, just follow this track, and you'll come to the boundary of the garden. You'll see the gable end of the house from there. Can't miss it.' He pushed his free hand into a pocket and pulled out an enormous key. 'Main door,' he told her, passing it over. 'We do have permission to view. See you soon.'

Annie watched them go. Mark had his arm round Enid now. Their heads were close together as he said something inaudible but obviously funny enough to make her giggle infectiously. She blinked the sudden sting of tears away and walked on, following the track, hating the way she seemed to cry so easily these days.

She'd imagined she'd done the right thing in coming here this weekend—tidying up loose ends, enabling her to draw a line under the part of her life that had been played out here with such devastating consequences. But being in the company of young lovers who had everything going for them only made her own loneliness and disillusionment more painful.

'Stop it!' she snapped at herself out loud. 'Just get a grip!' There was no one to hear her but the birds, and a stray rabbit or two, so her self-castigating lecture didn't embarrass her. 'So what if the only man you could ever love doesn't love you? If he thinks you're a gold-digging trollop and treated you accordingly. You got your revenge, didn't you? Reinforced his nasty opinion of you with interest—made it stick in his so-superior throat and choke him! It was your decision so you've got to live with it. At least it was a better option than hanging around, panting for whatever crumbs he decided to give you, wondering each day if this was going to be the day when he'd say, Nice knowing you, Annie Kincaid, and walk away.'

That brought her to the edge of the wood. A chestnut fence separated it from the gardens. She pushed through the wicket gate, feeling better for having got that lot out of her system, enabling her to enjoy this perfect day.

The heat of the summer was past, tempered by the sharper edge of autumn. The gardens, she noted, were a delight, despite recent neglect. Random planting of flowering shrubs, currant bushes and sprawling roses bordered overgrown grassy paths that led to odd-shaped lawns, and thickly planted herbaceous borders, where the glowing jewel shades of asters and sedums predominated now, in turn gave onto secret places, one garden room leading into another, and another—too many to explore right now.

Perhaps after that picnic lunch, she thought, heading for the house itself. A long, sprawling half-timbered Tudor house, oak-mullioned windows and a forest of huge ornamental brick chimneys. Lucky, lucky Enid!

She fitted the key into the lock and the heavy oak iron-studded door swung open easily. She hovered on the threshold, not daring to explore further because she knew the house was exactly what she would have wanted for herself—and she didn't want to get envious or self-pitying all over again.

She couldn't stand it!

She would go outside and wait for the others.

'Like it, Annie?'

Annie froze. She would know that voice anywhere. She suddenly felt as if she'd been left in a deep freeze for months on end. She couldn't move.

'Lost your voice?'

She wished he'd lost his! There should be a law against such sexy, gravelly tones! She turned with desperate reluctance, memories of their last meeting making her feel ashamed of herself, of the bravado that had seemed at the time the only possible solution, the only way to pay him back for his vile opinion of her, for the things he'd felt driven to do to protect his brother.

The sun was behind him; he was silhouetted in the doorway. Sheer male menace. 'I thought you were in Brussels.' If there was a note of accusation in her voice she could do nothing about it. He had, as far as she was concerned, no right to be here at all, spoiling her day. Spoiling her whole darned life, she amended bitterly.

'Of course you did. Otherwise you wouldn't be here now, would you?' He took a few steps into the panelled hall and Annie took a few steps back, halted by her eventual contact with the carved newel post of the staircase. 'But Mark wasn't lying to you. I was in Brussels on Thursday, when he gave you the invitation. I flew back last night and drove straight to the cottage.'

So he must have talked to Mark quite recently— since Thursday, anyway. Yesterday on the phone? Did it matter? The only thing to do was act as if his totally unexpected and completely and utterly unwanted presence was a matter of supreme indifference to her.

She would not let herself be embarrassed by the awful lies she'd told him, the way she'd rubbed his nose in the slime of his degrading opinion of her. She said coolly, 'You've timed your arrival well. The others will be here any second with the food and drink.'

He moved a little closer. Now that her eyes had grown accustomed to the interior dimness she could see he was smiling. That shattering half-smile that never failed to play havoc with her hormones. 'Not a chance,' he told her softly. 'By now they'll be well on their way, looking for another secluded place to have their picnic.'

It was several seconds before she could get to grips with that shocking revelation, then her mind ticked over furiously. Mark's insistence that his brother wouldn't be at his parents' home this weekend, the implication that he was stuck in Brussels for the duration. Mark's unease yesterday at the rain.

She understood that unease now. They could have still come here, of course, but in the car, not taking the scenic route through the woods. So they wouldn't have had the excuse of the forgotten picnic things to leave her on her own.

'Why?' she asked, shaken, as it all slotted into place, not understanding—needing to.

'I wanted to talk to you.'

'So?' She edged away, past the foot of the stairs, moving towards the big open fireplace. He followed her, pace for pace.

He was far too close. She was caught in the force field that surrounded him, drew her to him whether she willed it or not, made her think sinful thoughts. 'Couldn't you have gone through the normal channels? A phone call or a letter? Why this insane skulduggery—was Machiavelli a remote ancestor of yours?'

'If I'd phoned you'd have put the receiver down. If I'd written a letter you'd have torn it up. If I'd knocked on your door you'd have shut it in my face. You know you would, Annie, so stop quibbling. This seemed like the ideal opportunity to tell you what's in my mind—a five-minute walk away over the fields from my cottage, no door for you to slam in my face, nowhere for you to run to—you'd fall over your feet if you tried, looking at the size of those boots. My mother's, are they?'

She didn't bother to answer that, well aware of the large green rubber appendages on the end of her legs. 'What did you want to say to me that drove you to such devious lengths?' She headed for the door, trying not to give the demeaning impression that she was running away from him. Felt about half a per cent safer, more in control, as she gained it. But only until he slid an arm around her waist and dragged her down to sit beside him on the time-worn stone step.

'More a proposition, actually,' he drawled, pushing a tangle of escaping hair back from her face, tracing the outline of her cheek, watching her responsive shiver with narrow-eyed satisfaction. 'You can't deny what we do to each other. We rouse very strong emotions in each other—there's a two-way chemistry that makes it difficult to keep our hands off each other.'

He began to unbraid her hair. There was nothing she could do to stop him. She felt as if she'd been shot with a stun gun. Despite what she'd said to him, and the type of woman he believed her to be, did he want to continue their affair? Keep it secret, sordid?

What type of man did that make him?

He lowered his head until the sensual curve of his mouth was a breath away from hers, and the shudder that raced right through her went straight to the deepest places in her soul. The danger was immense. The danger that she would move the tiny fraction necessary to touch his lips with hers and in doing so negate all those stern lectures she'd given herself, the hard lessons she'd learned.

'This man you've decided to sell yourself to—the one you told me about, remember? Why go to him when you could have me? Well, I might not be as loaded as you say he is, but I've enough to see you don't starve, and I can give you good sex. I haven't got a title, but I could always buy one, so that wouldn't be a problem. I can't do anything about my age, I'm afraid, so unlike him I'm not likely—at least I hope not—to kick the bucket just yet and leave you to inherit all my worldly goods. But—'

Annie slapped him. Hard. Leapt to her feet, sobbing with fury. How dared he? Oh, how dared he! The hateful, hateful man!

His low, satisfied laughter followed her. She fell over her feet and sprawled inelegantly on the grass. Within seconds he'd picked her up, holding her against his heart until her storm of furious outrage died down enough for her to hear him when he said, 'Little liar! There never was an ancient titled Croesus just waiting to put his ring on your finger. You just proved it, my precious.'

'It was what you expected to hear!' she defended, scrubbing away the angry, humiliated tears, not willing to let herself be charmed back into his sexy web of deceit and double-dealing.

'No,' he denied seriously, catching her hands between his. 'It tore my world apart. Later, when I'd come to my senses and realised that hitting the bottle was no answer at all, I started to think. You said you were a clone of Lorna Fox, and for you to have known about her, what she was like, Mark had to have talked to you. He and I got together, and, yes, he *had* told you. He'd been trying to get you to find a way to forgive me for my behaviour on the night of Ma's party. He was horrified when he learned his information had done just the opposite.'

'That does not excuse the way you played me for a fool in Italy,' Annie reminded him gruffly.

'I did no such thing. I made love to you. We made love to each other.'

His words evoked memories that were too painful to bear. 'You took me to Italy thinking I was a gold-digging slag, and when we got there you took me to bed and treated me like one!'

He silenced her in the only way he knew how—kissing her until she was reeling, her breath sobbing in her lungs.

She was a total push-over where he was concerned, she told herself despairingly, shattered, leaning her burning forehead against his chest.

'Now will you just listen?' he demanded. He sounded breathless, too, and she could feel the drumbeat of his heart. Her head was spinning too wildly to let her formulate a single reasonable argument against doing any such thing.

'I know you've a lot to forgive me for, my sweet, but at least listen to my side of the story,' he pleaded. 'The very first time I saw you, at Edward Ker's retirement party, I wanted you. When you came out onto the terrace and into my arms I thought I'd gone to heaven. I didn't know why you'd done it, and when I'd come back down to earth I cynically came up with a few unpleasant answers. Then I heard Rupert had been dumped, and when you turned up that weekend with Mark I admit I thought the worst—that you were Lorna Fox Mark Two.'

His hands wandered over her slender back, soothing her, his voice self-denigrating as he told her, 'Tricking you into spending the night with me wasn't the act of noble duty I told myself it was. I wanted you for myself, so Mark couldn't have you. My head was in a mess. You'd got me so I wasn't capable of a single reasonable thought.

'I was telling myself not to let myself get involved while all the time I was wanting to. When I found odds and ends of your clothes stuffed in a drawer I had my opportunity. I went to Mark's office and told myself it was with the intention of calling you a blackmailing bitch—at the time you thought I was about to be married, remember?—but I ended up being jealous as hell when I saw you in Mark's arms and extending the invitation to travel to Italy to meet Roselli to you instead of to my brother.

'Again, the desire to keep Mark out of your clutches wasn't the prime motivation. I wanted you for myself. I'm not proud of myself, Annie.'

At least he was man enough to admit his sins, Annie thought. For a proud man, that must hurt. She wondered whether to tell him he'd made her love him, and rub salt in the wound, but decided she couldn't be that cruel.

The side of his face was resting against the top of her head, his hands tangling in the long cloak of her hair. Oh, if only they could always be this close, she mourned, but once he'd confessed his sins, unburdened himself, he would walk away. Five minutes over the fields, back to his cottage.

Would Mark and Enid come back for her? They'd all got together and planned how to get her in a position of having no option but to listen to him ease his conscience. They must really want him to be at peace with himself...

'In Italy we talked, and I got to know you. And I ended up falling in love with you, wanting you with me always. When I came to your flat, twenty-four hours after our return, I was going to ask you to marry me. I'd got the ring in my pocket and had made an offer for this house that no one could refuse. It's mine, as of yesterday. Ours, if you'll share it with me. Well, after you hit me with all that stuff it took me a few days to realise that the things you'd said had been nothing but a self-defensive pack of lies. So I'm asking you again: will you marry me, Annie?'

Her legs buckled. It was too much to take in. He really did love her. He'd remembered what she'd said about wanting a big rambly country house to put all her children in—their children! And had gone ahead and bought the perfect property!

His arms enclosed her more tightly, supporting her against his body. She lifted her face to his, tears falling from her pansy-purple eyes. He kissed them gently away. 'What a fool I've been!' she agonised. 'After what Mark told me about that woman I thought you were going to give me the brush-off. I couldn't bear it. I loved you so much it hurt. So I got in first and hurt you back, told those awful lies. I don't deserve you!'

'You deserve the very best, and I'll do my damnedest to reach that high standard,' he teased. He finished mopping up her tears with his lips and turned his attention to the corner of her soft, receptive mouth. 'You still haven't answered me. Will you marry me?'

'Oh, please!' She nibbled lovingly at his lower lip until, with a groan, he kissed her properly, his hands wandering over her luscious curves until the blood roared through her veins. She tugged him down onto the grass and he thrust one thigh between her legs. With unsteady fingers he began to prise open the buttons of her shirt.

She laid her hands against the lean, hard contours of his face, love soaring inside her, filling her with awe. He was truly hers. 'Love me for ever?' she whispered, and he raised his eyes from his tender task and looked deeply into hers.

'Until the end of the world,' he assured her. 'You'll never be alone again, my sweet. Not while I live and breathe.'

Which was all she wanted to know.

EPILOGUE

THREE weeks later the main bedroom in the penthouse suite of one of London's most exclusive and sophisticated hotels looked as if a bomb had hit it: feminine fripperies scattered everywhere, a wild jumble of make-up and perfumes, mountains of tissue paper.

And this was her wedding day.

Annie smiled beatifically at Enid and Cathy, who were helping each other into cream-coloured wild silk bridesmaid's dresses. Dear Daniel—darling, caring, wonderful, sexy, beloved Daniel—had insisted on booking them into this astronomically expensive suite, tolerating no arguments.

'I won't have my gorgeous bride and her attendants falling over each other in that poky Earl's Court flat—you can spend your pre-wedding night in luxury, have breakfast brought up to you in bed and indulge in all the girl-talk you want to in idleness and comfort. Besides, we're having the reception there.'

Oh, she couldn't wait to see him to tell him...!

Not long now, though. She'd phoned Mark's flat first thing, as soon as she'd discovered—Daniel had spent the night there; Mark was his best man—but Mark had said, 'No, you can't speak to him. He's in the shower. Besides, it's bad luck.'

'No, it isn't. Seeing each other is supposed to be

bad luck, not just speaking to each other—not that I believe that superstitious nonsense for a second.'

'Do not tell me,' Mark had said fiercely, 'that you're having second thoughts!'

'Of course not!'

'That's OK, then.' Mark had calmed down. 'It would finish him off if you were. Like me to give him a message?' he'd offered blandly.

She had to break the news in person! She'd huffed frustratedly down the phone, then said on a note of treacly sweetness, 'Nothing that's fit for his little brother's innocent ears! Just tell him I love him.'

Not long now, though!

Turning to the mirror, she inspected herself. Her newly washed hair looked wild, but there wasn't anything she could do to tame it. Daniel had forbidden her, ever, to strangle it back into a braid, and that was fine by her. And Enid and Cathy had done wonders with her make-up. Now all she had to do was get into that dress...

She picked it from its hiding place in the long, classy box she'd stuffed under the bed, and wriggled into it while the other girls were fixing each other's flowery coronets in place.

When they turned and saw her their mouths fell open.

Enid was the first to find her voice. 'You look stunning, absolutely stunning!'

'Oh, my God!' Cathy sounded as if an unseen hand was squeezing her windpipe. 'Do you believe it?' She turned to the grinning Enid. 'She very nearly had me fooled. Started dressing in prim and proper little suits and doing the housework—housework, would you credit it?—covered in a pinny! The leopard has *not* changed her spots!'

'Well, not all of them,' Annie admitted with a seraphic smile. Maybe she would dress more suitably, but she wouldn't throw her spotlight-grabbing clothes away; she'd keep them to dazzle Daniel with.

But never again would she be deliberately messy around the house. Bull Farm would be freshly decorated and furnished with the basics she and Daniel had already chosen on their return from honeymoon. She couldn't wait to transform the lovely old house into a cosy, welcoming home, to make life comfortable as well as special and exciting for her darling Daniel and—

A rap on the door heralded Mark's father, handsome in his morning suit. 'The cars are here—my word, Annie—you're a sight for old eyes!'

She smiled radiantly for him. Over the past three weeks she'd got to know him a whole lot better. And when he'd heard of her complete lack of family and offered shyly, 'May I have the privilege of giving you away, my dear?' she had accepted joyfully.

Pushing her feet into her high-heeled sandals, she picked up her bouquet and walked out on his arm, causing a small sensation as they passed through the main lobby to the waiting car. Annie held her head high. The marriage ceremony was made for solemn promises, but it was also a celebration, and she was going to play her part in that celebration to the hilt!

And she and Daniel had one extra, very special thing to celebrate...

* * *

As the great organ swelled into the traditional 'Wedding March' Daniel turned expectantly to watch his bride. His eyes widened, then narrowed, his mouth twitching in an otherwise perfectly straight face. Beside him, he heard Mark's breath whistle through his teeth.

She looked absolutely sensational!

The radiance of love lit her beautiful face, and her generous smile was wide enough to encompass the world and everyone in it. Her wild and glorious hair flowed right down her back, pulled back just a little at the sides to display large pearl and diamanté drop-earrings, and her sensually swaying body was a scandalous delight in scarlet silk that clung to every glorious curve, reached her ankles but left her smooth shoulders bare and whitely gleaming, dipping between her breasts to reveal a tantalising cleavage.

Pride, delight, drenching love filled him with something close to awe. She was a witch, and a wonder, and she was his!

As she reached his side he was, as ever, seduced by her perfume, her presence. His eyes, as he looked deep into hers, spoke of a love that was too overwhelming to be put into words, and she twined her slender fingers around his, her smile radiant as she lifted herself up on her toes and swayed her body against his, whispering ecstatically, 'Darling Daniel, we're pregnant! I found out this morning. Isn't it wonderful? I couldn't wait to tell you!'

'Sweetheart—' he uttered emotionally, and then he closed his arms around her and kissed her with a thoroughness that sent a ripple of laughter through the invited congregation. Oblivious to everything but his adored Annie, the precious gift she had brought him this day, he wondered if he had any right to be this blessed, this happy.

The vicar cleared his throat loudly and Mark dug him frantically in the ribs, and the Reverend Porter-Blane, his eyes twinkling, solemnly intoned, 'Dearly beloved, we are gathered...'

Passion

**Looking for stories that *sizzle?*
Wanting a read that has a little
extra *spice?***

**Harlequin Presents® is thrilled
to bring you romances that
turn up the heat!**

In March 1999 look out for:

The Marriage Surrender
by Michelle Reid
Harlequin Presents #2014

Every other month throughout 1999,
there'll be a **PRESENTS PASSION** book by one
of your favorite authors: Miranda Lee,
Helen Bianchin, Sara Craven and Michelle Reid!

*Pick up a **PRESENTS PASSION**—
where **seduction** is guaranteed!*

Available wherever Harlequin books are sold.

HARLEQUIN®
Makes any time special ™

Look us up on-line at: http://www.romance.net

HPPAS1-R

Looking For More Romance?

Visit Romance.net

Look us up on-line at: http://www.romance.net

Check in daily for these and other exciting features:

Hot off the press
View all current titles, and purchase them on-line.

What do the stars have in store for you?

Horoscope

Hot deals
Exclusive offers available only at Romance.net

Plus, don't miss our interactive quizzes, contests and bonus gifts.

PWEB

Don't miss your chance to read
award-winning author

PATRICIA POTTER

First Scottish historical romance

THE ABDUCTION

An eye for an eye. Clan leader Elsbeth Ker longed
for peace, but her stubborn English
neighbors would have none
of it—especially since the
mysterious Alexander had
returned to lead the
Carey clan. Now the
crofters had been
burned out, and the
outraged Kers demanded
revenge. But when Elsbeth faced her enemy,
what she saw in his steel gray eyes gave her pause....

Look for *THE ABDUCTION* this March 1999,
available at your favorite retail outlet!

HARLEQUIN®
Makes any time special ™

Look us up on-line at: http://www.romance.net   PHABDUCT

Look for a new and exciting series from Harlequin!

HARLEQUIN

Duets™

Two __new__ full-length novels in one book, from some of your favorite authors!

Starting in May, each month we'll be bringing you two new books, each book containing two brand-new stories about the lighter side of love! Double the pleasure, double the romance, for less than the cost of two regular romance titles!

Look for these two new Harlequin Duets™ titles in May 1999:

Book 1:
WITH A STETSON AND A SMILE
by Vicki Lewis Thompson
THE BRIDESMAID'S BET
by Christie Ridgway

Book 2:
KIDNAPPED? by Jacqueline Diamond
I GOT YOU, BABE by Bonnie Tucker

**2 GREAT
STORIES BY
2 GREAT
AUTHORS
FOR 1 LOW
PRICE!**

Don't miss it! Available May 1999 at your favorite retail outlet.

HARLEQUIN®
Makes any time special.™

Look us up on-line at: http://www.romance.net   HDGENR

Sultry, sensual and ruthless...

THE
AUSTRALIANS

Stories of romance Australian-style, guaranteed to fulfill that sense of adventure!

This April 1999 look for
Wildcat Wife
by Lindsay Armstrong

As an interior designer, Saffron Shaw was the hottest ticket in Queensland. She could pick and choose her clients, and thought nothing of turning down a commission from Fraser Ross. But Fraser wanted much more from the sultry artist than a new look for his home....

The Wonder from Down Under: where spirited women win the hearts of Australia's most independent men!

Available April 1999
at your favorite retail outlet.

HARLEQUIN®
Makes any time special™

Look us up on-line at: http://www.romance.net   PHAUS10

Race to the altar—
Maxie, Darcy and Polly are

The **HUSBAND** *Hunters*

in a fabulous new
Harlequin Presents® miniseries by

LYNNE GRAHAM

These three women have each been left a share of
their late godmother's estate—but only if they marry
withing a year and remain married for six months....

Maxie's story: **Married to a Mistress**
Harlequin Presents #2001, January 1999

Darcy's story: **The Vengeful Husband**
Harlequin Presents #2007, February 1999

Polly's story: **Contract Baby**
Harlequin Presents #2013, March 1999

Will they get to the altar in time?

Available in January, February and March 1999
wherever Harlequin books are sold.

HARLEQUIN®
Makes any time special ™

Look us up on-line at: http://www.romance.net   HPHH

Coming Next Month

HARLEQUIN PRESENTS®

THE BEST HAS JUST GOTTEN BETTER!

#2019 PACIFIC HEAT Anne Mather
Olivia was staying with famous film star Diane Haran to write her biography, despite the fact that Diane had stolen Olivia's husband. Now Olivia planned to steal Diane's lover, Joe Castellano, by seduction...for revenge!

#2020 THE MARRIAGE DECIDER Emma Darcy
Amy had finally succumbed to a night of combustible passion with her impossibly handsome boss, Jake Carter. Now things were back to business as usual; he was still a determined bachelor...and she was pregnant....

#2021 A VERY PRIVATE REVENGE Helen Brooks
Tamar wanted her revenge on Jed Cannon, the notorious playboy who'd hurt her cousin. She'd planned to seduce him, then callously jilt him—but her plan went terribly wrong: soon it was marriage she wanted, not vengeance!

#2022 THE UNEXPECTED FATHER Kathryn Ross
(Expecting!)
Mom-to-be Samantha Walker was looking forward to facing her new life alone—but then she met the ruggedly handsome Josh Hamilton. But would they ever be able to overcome their difficult pasts and become a real family?

#2023 ONE HUSBAND REQUIRED! Sharon Kendrick
(Wanted: One Wedding Dress)
Ross Sheridan didn't know that his secretary, Ursula O'Neill, was in love with him until his nine-year-old daughter, Katie, played matchmaker.... Then it was only a matter of time before Katie was Ross and Ursula's bridesmaid!

#2024 WEDDING FEVER Lee Wilkinson
Raine had fallen in love with Nick Marlowe, not knowing the brooding American was anything but available. Years later, she was just about to marry another man when Nick walked back into Raine's life. And this time, he *was* single!

HARLEQUIN CELEBRATES

FIVE DECADES OF ROMANCE

In April 1999,
Harlequin Love & Laughter shows you
50 ways to lure your lover as we
celebrate Harlequin's 50th Anniversary.

*Look for these humorous romances at your
favorite retail stores:*

50 WAYS TO LURE YOUR LOVER
by Julie Kistler

SWEET REVENGE?
by Kate Hoffmann

Look us up on-line at: http://www.romance.net   H50LL_L